Monday's child is fair of face,

Tuesday's child is full of grace,

Wednesday's child is full of woe,

Thursday's child has far to go,

Friday's child is loving and giving,

Saturday's child works hard for his living,

And the child that is born on the Sabbath day

Is bonny and blithe, and good and gay.

Anon.

Thursday's Child

Other books by Noel Streatfeild

Thursday's Child

by Noel Streatfeild

illustrated by Peggy Fortnum

RANDOM HOUSE NEW YORK

Dedicated to an American Pen Friend

Kathy Retan

with Love

Trade Binding—ISBN: 0-394-82096-7
Library Binding—ISBN: 0-394-92096-1
Library of Congress Catalog Card Number: 71-123073

Manufactured in the United States of America
First American Edition

Contents

To the reader of this book

This story is about two girls and two boys who live at the beginning of this century. Life was very different then from what it is now. But I hope you will find that, however different the conditions, the children behave and think exactly as you do today. For though seventy years ago is a long time, children as people, have not changed very much.

Noel Streatfeild

The Choice

Margaret had been discovering all her life that grownups were disappointing conversationalists. So now that she was ten she was quite prepared to carry on a conversation by herself. That January afternoon as she walked or, sometimes—forgetting it was a crime—skipped home beside Hannah, she argued about boots.

"I know you say and Miss Sylvia and Miss Selina say that boots are economical because they last longer but I don't think that's true. All the other girls at school wear shoes and they say they don't wear out quickly and they ought to know. And what nobody understands is what wearing boots does to me—they humiliate my legs. If I wasn't me but a different person they would humiliate me all over, but not even boots can do that. I am Margaret Thursday and unhumiliatable."

Hannah, her mind worrying round like a squirrel in a cage, had not been listening to a word Margaret said. Now she pulled her to a halt in a shop doorway.

"Let's have a look at you, dear. You are to have tea with the rector."

Hannah was a bony woman, made bonier by wearing long stiff all-embracing corsets which creaked. She had worked for Miss Sylvia and Miss Selina Cameron most of her life, having first come to the house when she was thirteen as a between maid. She had sobbed herself sick before she went, much to her mother's annoyance.

"Give over, do," she had said. "What have you to cry about with everything so nice?"

The "everything" had been packed in Hannah's wicker basket, material provided by Mrs. Cameron but sewn by Hannah and her mother. Such riches! Print dresses, black dresses for the afternoon, aprons, caps and, of course, an outfit for church on Sundays.

The Camerons had been kind to her, which was why Hannah had stayed with the family. There had been periods when she had got so far as walking-out with one or another of the men servants, but things had happened. First, Mr. Cameron had died. Mrs. Cameron was the helpless type and she had clung to Hannah, who had by then risen to being parlormaid, as though to a rock. For some reason, which Hannah had never understood, after Mr. Cameron's death there was less and less money. Slowly, changes had to be made. Not at once but over the years. First the men servants, then the cook and her assistants were given notice, until finally—except for a man once a week for the garden—there was only Hannah.

When Hannah had first come to work for the Camerons, Miss Sylvia had been twenty and Miss Selina eighteen. In those days they had been known as "those pretty Cameron girls." Now Hannah was over sixty, so Miss Sylvia was over seventy and Miss Selina rising seventy, and they were known as "the old Cameron ladies."

Hannah had carefully taught Margaret, almost since she was a baby, how to be a good housewife. Her efforts had little effect for Margaret loathed dusting, polishing and sweeping, and as for laundry she just would not try.

But Hannah's efforts were not altogether a failure for she had taught Margaret to cook. Often Hannah found herself so tired at the end of the day she could hardly drag herself up to bed, but it had never crossed her mind to give in her notice. Miss Sylvia, always the delicate one, was getting very frail, and poor Miss Selina ever so hazy in her mind. Anyway, Saltmarsh House, where they lived, was her home. She could not imagine living anywhere else.

Now Hannah's bony, work-roughened fingers attempted to tidy Margaret's hair. This was chestnut colored and very curly so not at all easy to control.

Margaret tried to wriggle out of Hannah's reach. She loved the rector but was surprised to be going to tea with him, for he was not the sort of man to give sudden invitations.

"Why am I going to tea with the rector?" she asked, still trying to pull away from Hannah. "Please leave my hair alone. You know the rector isn't the sort of person who cares how people look."

"Tidiness shows respect," said Hannah. She stood away from Margaret to see the whole effect. Margaret was dressed as simply brought-up children were dressed in the winter at the beginning of the century. A blue pleated skirt, a darker blue jersey and a red coat. On her head was a red tam-o'-shanter. On her legs black woolen stockings and the boots.

Hannah sighed, conscious that all Margaret's clothes were darned and could do with a sponge.

"I suppose you'll have to do, but if only we'd had warning you could have worn your Sunday green."

"Thank goodness you didn't know," said Margaret. "I

hate wearing my green for you've patched the elbows
with stuff that doesn't match."

Hannah gave her a sad smile.

"Beggars can't be choosers. Come on or I'll be late getting my ladies' teas."

Margaret liked going to the rectory for Mr. Hanslow,
the rector, was, excluding Hannah, her greatest friend.
The rectory could have been a beautiful house, but the
rector was very poor so both it and his garden were neglected. He was looked after by a Mr. and Mrs. Price who
lived in a cottage down the road. Mr. Price was really the
verger, but he managed to combine his church work with
a bit of gardening and cutting wood for the rector. Mrs.
Price cooked abominably and did what little housework
was done.

Margaret never rang the rectory bell, she just opened

the front door and shouted.

"Can I come in? It's me—Margaret."

The study door opened and the rector came smiling into the passage. He gave Margaret a kiss.

"There you are, my pet. Come in. Mrs. Price has made toast for our tea."

Over burnt toast and stewed tea, Margaret chattered away as usual, bringing the rector up to date with home and school news. Then, when Mrs. Price had cleared away the tea things, she stuck out her legs.

"Do you think you could speak to Miss Sylvia about these boots? Truly nobody wears boots any more. All the girls at school have laced-up shoes."

Mr. Hanslow did not look at the boots but straight into Margaret's eyes.

"I have always thought you were a sensible child, which is why I have asked you here today to discuss your future."

Margaret was surprised. What future? Nothing ever changed in Saltmarsh House. It must, she decided, be something to do with the little school for the daughters of gentlemen which she attended.

"Is it about school?"

"That is one of the things we have to talk about," said the rector. "You remember, of course, the details of how you came to live here."

Margaret was proud of her history.

"Of course I do. One Thursday you found me on the steps of the church when I was a teeny-weeny baby. And with me in my basket there were three of everything, all of the very best quality."

"And a note," the rector reminded her.

"Oh yes. Printed so no one would know who had written it. It said: 'This is Margaret, whom I entrust to your care. Each year fifty-two pounds will be sent for her keep and schooling. She has not yet been christened.' "

The rector nodded, smiling at the memory.

"You were a beautiful baby and if screams were anything to go by you certainly got the devil out of you at your christening. I would have dearly loved to take you in, but Mrs. Price could not sleep in and an old bachelor did not seem a suitable guardian for you, so . . ."

"So," Margaret prompted him, for she thought he was being rather slow telling the well-known story, "you asked the Miss Camerons to have me as they were the only people hereabouts with a big enough house and they said 'yes.' "

"God bless them," said the rector, "for there was no one else in the parish suitable and it did work out very nicely. But now things have gone wrong. This Christmas no money arrived for your keep."

"No money!" Margaret gasped, for always the money had arrived with the utmost regularity. It came each year between Christmas Eve and New Year's Day. It was put in a bag somewhere in the church—fifty-two golden sovereigns. The bag was never found in the same place twice and no one had ever seen the money arrive. "Do you think it came and someone stole it?"

The rector took a card out of his breast pocket and passed it to Margaret.

"This was found in the font."

Like the card which had come with her when she was a baby this one was printed. It said "NO MORE MONEY FOR MARGARET."

Margaret was shocked.

"How very mean! You would think a mother would manage something. Have you told Miss Sylvia and Miss Selina?"

The rector hesitated.

"Really this card has hastened something which had to happen sooner or later. Miss Selina is getting very old."

Margaret giggled.

"She's getting more and more like a baby every day. Now Hannah has to dress her and undress her."

"Very sad," said the rector, "but it is also very worrying. You see, with the old ladies needing so much attention, Hannah has too much to do. It has broken her heart to admit this but it is true. So even before Christmas I had agreed to find you a new home."

Margaret felt as Alice must have felt when she fell down the rabbit hole. A new home! But Saltmarsh House *was* her home, her only home. How could she be going to a new one—children never did that.

"I suppose you didn't know," she said, "but I help Hannah. Often and often I cook the supper and I do lots of other things—not as well as I cook, but I do them."

The rector took one of Margaret's hands.

"It is not a question of helping in the house, it's everything. The two old ladies are all Hannah can manage. She admitted this before Christmas and we discussed plans, thinking you still had an income of fifty-two pounds a year. But now the situation has changed. The Miss Camerons are, as you know, very far from rich, and now you have no money . . ." The rector broke off, looking at Margaret with great love but also with a child-like confusion.

The rector's worried face pulled Margaret together.

"If I still had fifty-two pounds a year where were you going to send me?"

"Nothing was decided, but we had thought of a boarding school."

"Well, I'm glad I haven't got the money for that for I'd hate it. Couldn't I live with you? I could do all the things Mrs. Price does and I'd work in the garden as well and I'd eat very little."

The rector looked more worried than ever.

"I thought of that, but Mrs. Price refused to consider it. She is a great sufferer with bad legs and . . ."

Margaret had her own views about Mrs. Price's bad legs, which she thought were used as an excuse not to work.

"Well send her away. I can look after both of us— truly I can."

The rector gave a little groan.

"It can't be done, pet. You see, there's Mr. Price. He doesn't really charge me, as you know, he throws me in, as it were, with his position of verger. I did speak to the archdeacon about you, asking his opinion as to whether you could possibly live here. But he said he thought an old bachelor like myself was a most unsuitable guardian for a little girl."

Margaret made a face.

"How silly of the archdeacon. Well, if I'm not staying at Saltmarsh House and I'm not staying here, where am I going?"

The rector had spent many hours on his knees asking God for advice and help in handling this interview. He was convinced help and advice would be given to him if only he was spiritually able to receive it. Now, with Margaret's brown eyes gazing up at him, he felt painfully inadequate and ashamed. Why was he so ineffectual a man that he had not risen in the world so that he had the wherewithal to help children such as Margaret?

"I'm afraid, pet, you are not going to care for either of the two solutions I have to offer. You are, I know, a brave child, but now you will need all your fortitude."

Margaret stiffened to take what was coming.

"Whatever it is," she said, "I'm still me—Margaret Thursday. Go on, tell me."

Since Margaret had no surname it was the rector who had chosen Thursday, the day on which he had found her. He thought it touching that she was so proud of it.

"I have, of course, tried everywhere to find you a home in this parish. I have succeeded in only one case. Your school. I know you do not much care for your teacher, but though perhaps she has a difficult nature she is a good Christian woman."

"I have never seen anything very Christian about her," said Margaret. "I think she's hateful."

The rector shook his head.

"You must not make such harsh judgments, pet, especially now that she is trying to help. She has offered you a home in the school. Her suggestion is that you should do school work in the mornings and housework in the afternoons and . . ."

But there the rector stopped for Margaret, her eyes flashing, had jumped to her feet.

"I'd never live there, I'd rather die. You should see that poor Martha who works there now. I think she beats her and there are black beetles in the kitchen. Anyway, do you think I'd be a maid in my own school where, whatever anybody else thinks, I know I'm not just as good as anybody else but a lot better? Remember I came with three of everything and of the very best quality."

The rector screwed himself up to tell Margaret his alternative suggestion.

"The archdeacon has told me of an institution of which his brother is a governor. It is an orphanage, but an exceptionally pleasant place I understand. He has offered to speak to his brother about you."

Margaret swallowed hard, determined not to cry.

"Where is it?"

"Staffordshire."

Margaret tried to recall the globe in the school classroom. She was now in Essex—surely Staffordshire was miles away.

"Near Scotland?" she suggested.

"Oh, not so far as that. The orphanage is near a town called Wolverhampton. I do not know it myself."

Margaret was so dispirited her voice was a whisper.

"Would they take me for nothing?"

"Yes."

"And I would be treated like all the other girls?"

"Girls and boys—orphanages take both."

Margaret gulped hard but she would not cry.

"Then that's where I'll go. If I can't stay here I'd rather go to a place where I am treated as a proper person."

Packing Up

The orphanage—called St. Luke's—was, so pamphlets pleading for funds said, "A home for one hundred boys and girls of Christian background." The building had been given and endowed by a wealthy businessman who had died in 1802. He had stipulated in his will that though the actual building was near Shrewsbury no child from any part of the country who was an orphan and a Christian was to be refused a vacancy provided he or she was recommended by a clergyman of the established church.

"So splendid of the archdeacon to recommend you," the rector said to Margaret, "for he carries more weight than I could hope to do, and then, of course, there is his brother who is a governor."

One of the worries of the committee who ran St. Luke's was how to collect their children. Most of them were too young to travel alone, especially as the journey included changing trains and crossing London. So a system had been devised by which new arrivals were collected in groups. When possible, new entrants were delivered to London by their relatives or sponsors, and there they were met by someone from the orphanage.

The rector came up to Saltmarsh House each time there was news about Margaret, but it was March before he arrived with definite information. Hannah always considered it unseemly that the rector should come into the kitchen, so he was led into the drawing room. It was cold, for neither Miss Sylvia nor Miss Selina came down until teatime so the fire was never lit until after luncheon.

"Stay and hear the news," the rector told Hannah, "for it concerns you." He opened a letter from the archdeacon and read: " 'I have now heard from the chairman of the committee of good ladies who run the domestic affairs of the orphanage. She says there are two members of one family to be admitted at the same time as your protégé Margaret Thursday. They are to meet in the third class waiting room at Paddington Station on the 27th of this month at 1 p.m. The train does not leave until 2:10, but the children will be given some sort of meal. They say Margaret Thursday should bring no baggage as all will be provided.' "

Hannah was appalled.

"No baggage indeed! That's a nice way for a young lady to travel. Margaret came to us with three of everything and she is leaving us the same way, not to mention something extra I've made for Sundays."

"I think," the rector explained, "the orphans wear some kind of uniform."

"So they said on that first form they sent," Hannah agreed, "but there was no mention of underneath." Then she blushed. "You will forgive me mentioning such things, sir."

The rector dropped the subject of underneath.

"Do you think arrangements could be made for someone to stay with your ladies for one day while you take

Margaret to Paddington Station? I would take her myself, but the archdeacon says . . ." He broke off, embarrassed. Hannah understood.

"No, better I should go. It's not a gentleman's job. We'll have to book on the carrier's cart to the railway junction for London."

The rector was glad to do something.

"I shall see to that, indeed I will arrange everything. All you have to do is to be ready by the 27th. Can you manage that, Margaret, my pet?"

Margaret had been waiting for a chance to speak.

"Can I take my baby clothes with me?"

"Whatever for?" gasped Hannah.

"I don't quite see . . ." the rector started to say, but Margaret interrupted him.

"I don't want to get to this St. Luke's looking like a charity child. If I show my baby clothes—three of everything and of the very best quality—they'll know I'm somebody."

The rector looked at Margaret's flashing eyes. He spoke firmly for he wanted her to remember his words.

"If you behave like somebody you will be treated like somebody. Never allow anyone to suggest that because you do not know who your parents were you are in any way inferior to others more fortunately placed."

"You needn't worry," said Margaret. "I never will. But I think it will help if everybody can see I'm someone who has a mother who cared that her baby was properly dressed. How can people know that if they don't see the clothes?"

The rector held out a hand to Margaret and she came to him.

"It is my hope that someday your mother will come and claim you. You do not know and I do not know what terrible thing happened to her that forced her to leave her baby on the church steps. Nor do we know what new misfortune has deprived her of money. But I believe— and I pray for this night and morning—that one day her fortunes will change and then she will come to me and say: 'Where is my Margaret?' Then I shall ask: 'First, madam, describe the baby clothes you left for the child, otherwise how do I know you are her mother?' "

"Well, truthfully," said Margaret, "it's not likely the wrong mother would want me. What for?"

The rector smiled.

"How do we know?" he teased her. "Someday you may prove to be the heir to a great fortune. Remember, Thursday's child has far to go."

"Or," Hannah suggested, "you might become famous. I'm always telling her, sir, she might write a book. You ought to hear the stories she tells me of an evening, and all out of her head."

"So you see," said the rector, "I must keep the baby clothes for the day when your mother claims you." He got up. "Now I must get on with your affairs. I will arrange for the carrier to call here on the 27th."

Hannah still had the wicker basket which she had brought to Saltmarsh House, and now she gave it to Margaret. To make her an "underneath" trousseau she had raided the old ladies' cupboards. There she had discovered an unused length of flannel, a voluminous cambric petticoat, and other useful bits and pieces. She had sewn the clothes at night after Margaret was in bed, so it was the night before she left that Margaret saw them for

the first time after they were packed in the wicker basket.

"Three of everything," Hannah said proudly, lifting layers of tissue paper. "Three plain cambric petticoats. Three pairs of drawers with featherstitching. Three scalloped flannel petticoats. Three linings in case at that orphanage they make you wear dark knickers. Three liberty bodices and three nightdresses—all fine tucked." Then Hannah drew back yet one more piece of tissue paper. "And here for Sundays is a petticoat and a pair of drawers edged with lace."

Margaret gasped. Then she threw her arms around
Hannah.

"Lace! Oh, darling Hannah, thank you. It's like being
a princess. When we go to church on Sundays I'll be sure
to see that my frock sticks on my heel so everyone can see
the lace."

Hannah was shocked.

"You'll do nothing of the sort. Remember, you were
spoke for by an archdeacon, so don't shame him." Then
she turned back to the wicker basket. "Your Bible and
prayer book are in the bottom. I've tucked your stockings
in wherever there is room, but on the top are your
hankies, your brush and comb, your toothbrush and one
nightie so you can get at them easy if you arrive late. And
in a corner down at the bottom is that tin of mine with
the cat on it you're so fond of. I've filled it with toffees."

Suddenly it all seemed terribly final. Although one
part of Margaret had accepted the fact that she was going
to the orphanage, another part of her had refused to believe it. Could she really be going away from the rector
and Hannah and all the people she knew and loved?
With a howl she threw herself at Hannah.

"Must I go? I'll work in the house much more than I
ever did before. I'll like dusting, truly I will, and I'll
hardly eat anything at all."

Hannah, her eyes dimmed by tears, gave Margaret a
little push.

"Don't, my darling. Don't. It won't do no good." Then
she knelt down and closed the wicker basket and fastened
a leather strap around it.

The Journey

The orphanage was poor. The endowment, which a hundred years before had seemed more than sufficient to dress, feed and house a hundred orphans, was now quite inadequate. Charitable people subscribed and sometimes held bazaars and jumble sales to raise funds, but there was still barely enough to keep the home going. The matron, who was a hard woman and in any case disapproved of spoiling orphans, kept the expenses down by saving on food. "What won't fatten will fill" was one of her favorite sayings. As a result, Miss Jones, called assistant nurse but really assistant everything who had been sent to meet Margaret and the other children, was very conscious of the lightness of the bag containing her own and the orphans' dinners to be eaten in the waiting room. A stale loaf of bread, some margarine and one ounce of cheese per person and a bottle of water.

Miss Jones was already in the waiting room when Hannah and Margaret arrived. She scarcely looked at them but fixed horrified eyes on the wicker basket.

"I hope that is not the child's luggage. You were informed no luggage was to be brought."

Hannah had sized up Miss Jones. "That's a jumped-up Miss Nobody," she thought. Out loud she said:

"No young lady I have charge of goes away without baggage and don't forget, Margaret is no common orphan. She was spoken for by the archdeacon whose brother is one of the orphanage governors."

Miss Jones never saw the governors—her life was ruled by Matron, of whom she was terrified. But it was common knowledge in the orphanage that even Matron had to listen to the governors. Perhaps if this child—to whom she had taken an instant dislike—knew a governor it was better to leave the question of her baggage to Matron. She looked coldly at Margaret.

"You are, I suppose, Margaret Thursday."

"That's right," Margaret agreed. "Of course, Thursday isn't my real name. I was called that because that was the day the rector found me and . . ."

Miss Jones pointed to the bench on which she was sitting.

"That's enough talking, sit down quietly." Then she said to Hannah: "You can go now."

Both Margaret and Hannah forgot Miss Jones. They gazed at each other with stricken faces.

"Oh, my dear pet!" said Hannah, holding out her arms. "Oh, my dear pet!"

Margaret put down the basket and ran to her.

"Hannah! Hannah! Don't leave me."

Hannah, with tears rolling down her face, knelt and hugged her.

"You have some stamps the rector gave you," she whispered. "Bear it if you can, dear, but if you can't, write and something might be thought of."

Margaret hugged Hannah tighter.

"Don't leave me. You can't! You can't!"

Hannah knew that every minute she stayed made things worse for Margaret. She freed herself from her clinging arms and, blinded by tears, stumbled toward the door. Margaret tried to run after her, but Miss Jones grabbed her by the wrist and picked up the wicker basket.

"Sit down and behave yourself. I never saw such a display. You wait until Matron hears of this."

"Hannah! Hannah!" screamed Margaret.

But Hannah was gone and the door had shut behind her.

Miss Jones was furious. There were others in the waiting room and they were looking pityingly at Margaret. It was too much, making her look like the wicked stepmother in a fairy tale when really she should be admired.

"Be quiet," she said in an angry whisper. Then, raising her voice for the benefit of the others in the room: "This is a very ungrateful way to behave for you are a lucky girl to be going to St. Luke's."

At that moment there was a diversion. The waiting-room door opened and three more children came in—a girl and two boys. They were shabbily dressed in black and each was as golden-haired as Margaret was brown. The eldest, who was the girl, led her brothers toward Miss Jones. In spite of the shabby clothes, the girl had evidently known better days for she spoke in the clear voice of the well-educated.

"Are you the lady from St. Luke's?"

Miss Jones nodded and said, "You must be the three Beresford children."

"That is correct," the girl agreed. "I am Lavinia. This"—she pulled the elder boy forward—"is Peter, and this"—she tried to pull forward her younger brother—"is Horatio." But Horatio refused to be pulled.

"Don't like that lady," he announced. "Horry wants to go home."

Miss Jones made tch-tching noises. This really was her unlucky day. Now another child was going to make a scene. But she had reckoned without Lavinia. She let go of Horatio's hand, felt in her coat pocket, and brought out a sweet and put it in the little boy's mouth.

"You mustn't mind him," she told Miss Jones. "He's little, but he'll settle down."

Miss Jones opened her coat to look at her watch, which was fixed to her blouse with a gun-metal bow. Thankfully she saw it was time to eat.

"Now sit down, all of you, and have some dinner. We have a long journey ahead of us." She opened the dinner bag and took out the food and a knife. She cut five slices of bread, smeared on a little margarine, then placed a small knob of very dry cheese on each slice. She passed one to each of the children. Horatio looked at his in disgust.

"Is this meant to be dinner?" he asked.

Lavinia put an arm around him.

"Eat it, darling," she whispered. "Then you shall have a sweet."

Margaret had received her slice but she made no effort to eat. She had succeeded in stopping crying except for an occasional hiccuping sob, but she had such a lump in her throat she knew she couldn't swallow anything.

Lavinia, taking advantage of a moment when Miss Jones was repacking the food and the knife, leaned across to Peter.

"Put the little girl's slice in your pocket," she whispered. "She'll be hungry later on."

Somehow the other children had got their food down. Miss Jones took another look at her watch. She got up.

"Come along," she said. "Pick up that basket, Margaret, and hold my hand. You three," she told the Beresfords, "follow me and be sure to keep close."

In the train Margaret began to feel better. Presently she felt so much better she was able to eat her bread and cheese, now rather hairy after being in Peter's pocket. They had a reserved compartment and Miss Jones sat in a corner as far from the children as possible, so in a whisper Lavinia and Margaret exchanged information.

"I'm not going to St. Luke's except for a few days," Lavinia explained. "There were only vacancies for the boys. Anyway I'm fourteen so I'm going into service somewhere near so I can see the boys on my half days."

Margaret could not imagine Lavinia in service. She wasn't a bit like Hannah or that poor Martha at the school.

"Will you like being in service?"

"I want to learn how to run a house," Lavinia explained.

Peter broke in. "Our mother said you could never give orders if you didn't know how a house should be run."

Margaret had not supposed orphans gave orders, so Peter's statement cheered her. She knew that she would be a giving-orders sort of person, but it was nice to think she would not be alone. Then she had another cheering thought. Perhaps if she made friends with these children Lavinia would see her as well as her brothers on her half days.

"I'm ten, nearly eleven," Peter told her. "How old are you?"

"I'm nearly eleven too," said Margaret. "How old is he?" She pointed to Horatio.

"It's rude to point," said Horatio, "but if you want to know I'm six."

Peter was determined that Margaret should be well informed.

"Our mother's dead," he announced.

"Yes, I suppose she is, and your father too," Margaret agreed, "or you wouldn't be orphans."

Peter started to answer that, but Lavinia evidently didn't want him to.

"No, we wouldn't be, would we? Now tell us about you."

"Well," said Margaret, "I'm not properly an orphan. I was found on a Thursday in a basket on the church steps with three of everything of the very best quality."

The Beresfords were thrilled.

"How romantic!" said Lavinia.

Peter looked admiringly at Margaret.

"So you could be absolutely anybody?"

"That's right," Margaret agreed. "And until this Christmas every year gold money was left in the church in a bag to keep me."

"And nobody saw who left it?" Lavinia asked.

"Never."

"My goodness," said Peter, "it's like a book!"

Lavinia looked across at Miss Jones and saw that she was asleep.

"Peter is going to write books when he grows up," she whispered to Margaret. "He's very clever. He never stops reading."

"I keep hoping there'll be books in the orphanage," said Peter, "then I won't mind how awful it is."

Horatio looked as though he might cry.

"It won't be awful, Vinia, will it?"

Lavinia sighed.

"Why did you say that?" she said to Peter. "Now he's going to cry and I've no sweets left."

That was Margaret's moment. She climbed quietly up on the seat and took her wicker basket off the rack.

"But I have," she said. "A whole box of toffees. Let's share them before she wakes, for I bet they won't let us eat them when we get there."

The Orphanage

The train did not arrive at Wolverhampton until nearly six o'clock and then there was a long drive in a horse-drawn omnibus. As a result the children, who since breakfast had only eaten the slice of bread and the morsel of cheese, and the few toffees, were so exhausted that they scarcely took in the orphanage.

To make everything more muddling the orphans appeared to be wearing fancy dress. They were having supper when the children first saw them. Forty-nine girls at one table, forty-eight boys at another, eating, the children noticed sadly, only bread and margarine and drinking what looked like cocoa.

"Oh dear!" Lavinia whispered to Margaret. "I did hope it would be soup and perhaps eggs."

The "fancy dress" was, the children were to learn, ordinary orphanage wear. It had been designed when the orphanage had first opened over a hundred years before and had never been changed. For the girls there were brown cloth dresses to the ankles, white caps and long aprons. For the boys there were loose brown trousers and short matching coats. Out-of-doors both girls and boys wore brown capes. On Sundays the girls had white muslin scarves folded into their dresses and the boys wore white collars.

That first night the children seemed to see nothing but brown everywhere they looked—brown out of which rose the noticeably pale faces of the orphans. As the children stood in the doorway swaying with tiredness and hunger, they were startled by the harsh voice of the matron.

"Don't stand there gaping, sit down. There is room for you two boys there and you girls here."

Lavinia pulled herself together.

"I think perhaps," she suggested in her quiet but authoritative voice, "I had better sit beside my little brother just for tonight. He is so tired he may need some help . . ."

She got no further for she was confronted by Matron, a stout woman who looked as if she had been poured into her black dress. She had sandy reddish hair and a fierce red face.

"I am matron here, young woman," she said, "and I give the orders. Off you go, boys, and you two girls sit. And do not forget to thank God for your good food."

The bread was stale and hard to get down, but the children were ravenous, and the cocoa—if it was cocoa for it tasted of nothing—was hot.

"We can have two slices each," a little girl next to Margaret whispered to her, "and sometimes, if there's any left over, a drop more cocoa."

Lavinia strained around to see how Horatio was getting on. Fortunately he was not crying for he was nearly asleep, but he was swallowing the pieces of bread soaked in cocoa which Peter was pushing into his mouth. Then she saw that Miss Jones, who was talking to Matron, was pointing to Margaret.

"Expect a storm," she whispered to Margaret. "I've a feeling Miss Jones is telling Matron about your basket."

Miss Jones was, and presently Matron came striding over to Margaret, her black upholstered chest heaving with what appeared to be rage. She clapped her hands.

"Silence, everybody," she roared. "What, children, is the orphanage rule about luggage?"

"Bring no luggage," the children chanted. "Everything needed will be provided."

"And is it provided?" Matron asked.

"Yes," answered the children.

"But here we have a new orphan who has quite deliberately disregarded the committee's rule." Matron beckoned to Miss Jones. "Bring Margaret Thursday's basket."

Miss Jones—a much meeker Miss Jones than the one who had met the children—scuttled out and was soon back carrying, as if it were a bomb, Hannah's wicker basket. At the sight of it in Miss Jones's arms, Margaret nearly broke out crying. Was it only last night that Hannah had so proudly shown her what she had packed? Lavinia slipped a hand into Margaret's.

"Don't give Matron the pleasure of seeing that you mind. I bet she likes seeing people cry."

Clearly Matron was surprised, in fact almost pleased, at the beautifully made and packed clothes. She had placed the basket on the end of the girls' table and had tossed aside the tissue paper. But as she took out one garment after another she made no comment except an occasional mutter to Miss Jones. "Ridiculous." "Much too good for an orphan." And finally, "Lace! Look, Jones, lace!" But as she repacked the little basket she laid a few things to one side.

"Come here, Margaret," she said.

Giving Margaret's hand a last squeeze, Lavinia moved to let Margaret get off the bench. Margaret, having scrambled over the bench, raised her chin in the air and marched over to Matron.

"I have not yet decided what shall be done with these clothes, but you may keep your Bible and prayer book and your toothbrush. What is this tin for?"

Matron held out the now empty toffee tin. The much-loved cat's head seemed almost to smile at Margaret. She swallowed a sob.

"It's to keep things in. It was a good-by present."

Perhaps because she had no use for it, for it could not have been kindness, Matron laid the tin beside the Bible, prayer book and toothbrush.

"You can go back to your seat. Take these things with you. Now stand, children. Grace."

The orphans pushed back the benches and stood, hands folded, heads bent. Then they sang Bishop Ken's Doxology.

"Praise God, from Whom all blessings flow,
Praise Him, all creatures here below,
Praise Him above, ye heavenly host,
Praise Father, Son and Holy Ghost."

"Yes, indeed," said Matron. "Never forget how fortu-

nate you are and how much you have for which to praise
God. See them up to the dormitories, Jones, but leave
Lavinia Beresford with me."

"Oh, couldn't I see Horatio to bed?" Lavinia pleaded.
"He's so little and so tired."

From the tone of Matron's voice, Lavinia might have
suggested having a bath in public.

"Go into the boys' dormitory! Are you mad, girl?
Quick, children, march."

The boys went first, each one as he passed Matron
bowing his head as if before a shrine. At the end, dragged
along by Peter, came Horatio. He was, Lavinia saw,
really walking in his sleep so he at least would not suffer.

The girls followed the boys, but they, as they passed Matron, each had to curtsy.

"I won't curtsy to anybody," Margaret muttered to Lavinia.

"Don't be a fool," Lavinia retorted. "What is the point of putting her back up?"

Margaret respected Lavinia's opinion and anyway she was too tired and too miserable to have much fight in her. So, clutching her possessions, she followed the last girl and, in spite of having her arms full, succeeded in making the necessary bob.

"I don't like the look of that girl," Matron observed to Miss Jones, who was following the children. "She has a proud air and must be humbled."

"Quite so, Matron," Miss Jones agreed. "I thought the same the moment I saw her, and the scene she made in the waiting room was disgraceful."

Lavinia followed Matron into her sitting room. It was, she noticed, a surprisingly comfortable room to find in that desolate place, and though it was March there was a cheerful fire burning in the grate. Drawn up to the fire was a table laid for a meal. Evidently, thought Lavinia, she is going to have her supper. Matron sat down at her table, but she did not ask Lavinia to sit.

"I have good news for you," she said. "The Countess of Corkberry, who has always taken a kindly interest in this place, needs a scullery maid. You are to receive five pounds a year, but her ladyship has agreed to advance part of that sum so that you may have a respectable wardrobe. I understand you have a tin trunk at the railway station. Does it contain any clothes suitable for a scullery maid?"

"I don't really know what a scullery maid wears," Lavinia confessed, "but I have some plain frocks. Perhaps they will do."

"Nonsense!" said Matron. "You will need print dresses, aprons and caps and a black outfit for Sundays. All the staff have to attend church." She looked at Lavinia's fair plaits. "And of course you must put your hair up."

"My hair up!" Lavinia gasped. "I'm only just fourteen."

"Fortunately in sewing classes our girls work at wardrobes for our leavers who are going into service, so you can be fitted out—at your expense, of course. I should think two days will be enough to provide everything. A carrier will bring your box here tomorrow."

"Two days!" said Lavinia. "I had hoped perhaps a week to see the boys settled in."

"Two days," said Matron. "We have no room for you here. For tonight a mattress has been put on the floor at the end of the girls' dormitory . . ." Matron stopped for there was a knock on the door. "Come in."

The knock had been made by a girl who looked no older than Margaret. She was wearing the orphanage uniform but her hair was screwed up inside her cap. She was carrying a laden tray.

"Ah, Winifred! Supper," said Matron. "Good."

Winifred put in front of Matron a large steak, a dish of potatoes and another of cauliflower. Then from a cupboard she fetched a bottle of porter.

Lavinia felt saliva collecting in her mouth at the sight of such good food.

"That will be all, Lavinia," said Matron. "Winifred

will direct you to the girls' dormitory."

Margaret, shivering with tiredness and lack of food, had accepted without question the bed pointed out to her. She had followed the other girls into an inadequate washroom in which were jugs of cold water and tin basins, into one of which they all cleaned their teeth. She had been shown a tiny shelf over her bed on which she was told to put her toothbrush and mug, her Bible and prayer book.

"And when Miss Jones says 'Pray' you stop whatever you are doing and kneel by your bed," her guide whispered, "or she hits you with a hairbrush."

Margaret had just pulled on the ugly coarse grayish-colored nightdress, which was lying on her bed, when the order came for prayer. She hurriedly dropped to her knees and buried her face in her hands. Evidently it was Miss Jones who decided how long prayers should be, for a few moments later there was another bark from her. "Up, girls, and into your beds."

Margaret had hidden the tin Hannah had given her in her bed. In the dark she hugged it to her. It was a little bit of Hannah. Putting her head under the scratchy inadequate bedcothes, she stifled her sobs.

"I can't bear it. They've taken all my clothes. I'll never wear lace on Sundays. Oh, Hannah! Hannah!"

But when a little later Lavinia crept up to the dormitory, Margaret, though her face was wet with tears, was asleep.

First Day

When Margaret woke up the next morning she could not
at first think where she could be. Accustomed to a room
of her own, she was puzzled by the sleeping sounds which
came from the orphans. Then, as if a cold heavy weight
had dropped onto her solar plexus, she remembered.
This was the orphanage. St. Luke's orphanage that the
archdeacon had told the rector was "an exceptionally
pleasant place." Pleasant! Rage filled Margaret. Then
she remembered she had three carefully hidden stamps.
Wait until she wrote to the rector and told him what
the archdeacon had dared to describe as exceptionally
pleasant.

Margaret sat up and looked down the dormitory.
There was not much light because the curtains were
drawn, but peering over the twenty-five beds which lined
each wall she could see at the far end of the room a mattress on the floor covered, as were the beds, with a gray
blanket. "That," she thought, "must be Lavinia. I bet
she won't mind if I wake her up."

To think of something meant for Margaret doing it

immediately. In a second she was out of her bed and, holding up her long grayish nightgown, was running down the dormitory. She sat down by the hump under the blanket which was Lavinia.

"Lavinia! Lavinia! Wake up. It's me. Margaret. What shall I do? I can't stay in this dreadful place. You won't leave Peter or Horatio here, will you?"

Lavinia had the gift of waking up clear-headed.

"You better go back to your bed," she whispered. "I'm sure you aren't allowed to be here."

Up went Margaret's chin.

"I don't care. I'm doing no harm. Did you hear what I said? I'm running away. I can't stay here."

Lavinia sat up.

"I'm only going to be here for two days. I'm to be scullery maid for somebody called the Countess of Cork-berry."

"Two days!" said Margaret. "I thought you said a week."

"I did, and that's what I hoped, but it's not to be. I'll be back every other Sunday."

"They said you could?"

Lavinia spoke with quiet authority.

"Either I have every other Sunday or I won't work for the Countess."

Margaret looked approving. That was the way to talk.

"I wish I could be a scullery maid. I'm a good cook and it's sure to be better than being here because it couldn't be worse."

"Well, you can't be," said Lavinia, "you're too young. You would have to pass a labor exam before you could go out to work. I quite see that you want to run away, but please stick it out for a bit. You see, I want you to keep an eye on Peter and Horatio."

Margaret weakened. She wanted to leave that morning. But perhaps she could bear a week or two, especially knowing Lavinia would come back every other Sunday.

"Well, I might stick it out for a bit, but . . ."

Margaret got no further for Miss Jones had flung open the door and was clanging a huge bell. She stopped in mid-clang, her mouth gaping, unable to believe her eyes.

"Margaret Thursday! What are you doing out of bed?"

Margaret got to her feet.

"Talking to Lavinia. She's my friend."

"Go back to your bed at once," Miss Jones thundered. Then she gave another clang on the bell. "Up, girls, up. Form a line for the washroom." She looked again at Margaret, who had not moved. "Now what is it?"

"You said I was to go back to bed. Then you said 'Up, girls, up,' and now you say form a line for the washroom. What do you want me to do?"

Miss Jones was more sure than ever that she did not like Margaret Thursday.

"You will get your toothbrush and mug and join that line there for the washroom."

It was a slow shuffling walk to get washed, made the more dismal by the shrieks of the small children who were being washed by Miss Jones and an assistant.

"They put soap in their eyes," a small girl who was in front of Margaret told her. "It happens every day. It used to happen to me."

"Beasts!" said Margaret.

Lavinia, who had taken her place behind Margaret, whispered: "I do hope Peter has managed to wash Horry.

He'd kick anyone who put soap in his eyes."

Margaret found that her clothes had disappeared and in their place were her orphanage clothes: a vest, a bodice, coarse long straight-legged drawers, a gray petticoat, the uniform dress, an apron and a cap. The only thing left of her own clothes were her boots.

"It would be them," she thought resentfully. Then there were tears in her eyes. Even the despised boots were something of home.

None of the clothes were new and none fitted, but Margaret was given some good advice by an older girl whom Miss Jones sent to show her how the uniform cap should be worn.

"Don't say anything doesn't fit," she whispered, "for you'll be made to alter it yourself in what they call 'free time'—we don't get much of that."

There was no such thing as a looking-glass in the dormitory, so Margaret could only guess at her appearance.

She could see, however, how the others looked and that was enough.

"My goodness!" she thought. "Suppose Hannah could see me now!"

As a matter of fact, Margaret was wrong. Of course the clothes were a century out of date so they felt ridiculous to her, used to skirts to her knees, but grown-up people thought the orphanage children looked picturesque. The cap really did suit Margaret. It was made of white cotton with a draw string at the back which held it tightly in position. The children were supposed to pull back their hair out of sight under the caps, but Margaret's curls refused to be controlled and spiraled out around her face.

Breakfast was another depressing meal. Each child had a bowl of lumpy porridge served with a mere splash of milk and no sugar. This was followed by one slice of bread and margarine and a cup of weak tea.

The orphans were not taught in the orphanage but, wrapped in their brown cloaks, were marched two-and-two down to the village school.

"At school don't they laugh at us in these clothes?" Margaret asked Susan, the girl who was paired with her.

Susan shook her head.

"No. They're used to us, and anyway I think they are sorry for us. Sometimes they give us things. Once I had a whole apple."

Margaret, used to the large overgrown garden at Salt-marsh House where fruit was to be had for the picking, felt even more depressed. Imagine speaking of an apple like that—something to be remembered!

"Don't we ever get fruit at the orphanage?"

"Oh yes," said Susan. "Always at Christmas we are

given an orange."

An orange! It was not just the fact that an orange a year was all she could expect, but Susan's calm acceptance that outraged Margaret. But she had other questions to ask. One had been worrying her since she had been given her uniform for nobody could run far dressed in it.

"What do they do with our own clothes?"

Susan looked scared, peering round to see that Miss Jones was not within hearing distance.

"We don't know."

"But they must be kept somewhere."

Susan whispered so low that Margaret had to strain to hear. "Some of them say Matron sells them."

"For herself?"

Susan nodded.

"But that's only what they say. We don't know."

"They won't sell mine," said Margaret. "I'll ask Matron for them."

Susan clutched at Margaret's arm.

"Don't. Just asking would mean a terrible punishment, you could . . ."

They were outside the school playground. Miss Jones, red-faced, was standing by Susan.

"What were you saying? You know talking is forbidden."

Susan might look meek, but she evidently knew how to fool Miss Jones.

"I was only telling Margaret what work we shall do in school this morning."

"Oh!" Miss Jones turned away. "Quick march. Straight to your classrooms. No playing in the yard."

School

A Miss Snelston was head of the village school and from the first the children liked her. It was not easy with only one pupil-teacher to assist her to teach children of all ages in two rooms, but somehow she managed.

Most of the pupils other than the orphans were the children of farm laborers. Red-cheeked, they were solidly built on a diet largely composed of vegetables, eggs, milk and bread, for at that time farm laborers' wages were very low so meat was a rarity. All the children, urged on by their parents, had one aim which was to pass the labor exam as early as possible so that the girls could go into service and the boys get work on the farms. Miss Snelston, of course, knew this was their ambition and she accepted it. "After all," she would say to her pupil-teacher, Polly Jenkin, "they may as well leave when they are twelve for you and I know that however long we keep them here, very few would learn any more, and of course it's hard for the parents to find the school money." School money was twopence a week, which in those days was paid as school fees.

It was Miss Snelston's hope each time there was a new batch of orphans that a really intelligent child would turn up. That was how she had found Polly Jenkin. She had taught her since she came to the orphanage at the age of four and had discovered in her a real fondness for learning, so the moment she passed her labor exam she had applied to the governors for her. She arranged that Polly was to receive two-and-sixpence a month and live in her cottage, in return for which she would help with the housework.

The school morning started with prayers and a hymn. Then, leaving Polly to get the school work started, Miss Snelston called Margaret, Peter and Horatio into her little office and gave them their slates.

"These are your very own," she explained. "You must look after them carefully for on them you do your sums and sometimes dictation. My aim is to see four sums right on every slate." She smiled at the three children, hiding from them her deep pity for well she knew how hard their lives would be. "You," she said to Peter, "must be Peter Beresford and this must be Horatio."

Horatio, looking very tiny in his brown uniform, which was at least two sizes too large for him, smiled back at Miss Snelston.

"That man that washed me put soap in my eyes," he told her.

"I'm sure he did," Miss Snelston thought, looking at Horatio's still bloodshot eyes and tear-stained cheeks. She turned up the sleeves of his jacket which entirely hid his hands.

"Dear me, that suit is very big for you." She turned to

Peter. "Bring him in here in middle morning break and
I'll stitch the sleeves up." Then she looked at the trousers
flapping around the child's ankles. "Do you think Matron would mind if I shortened the trousers?"

Peter was a good-looking boy with large blue eyes.
Now he turned these anxiously toward Margaret.

"Would she mind?"

Margaret felt something she had never felt before. A
sort of warm feeling around her heart. All her life people
had looked after her, and now somebody needed her. It
was nice to be needed.

"I shouldn't think she'd notice."

Miss Snelston evidently thought that sensible.

"You are Margaret Thursday?"

"That's right," Margaret agreed. "It's not my real surname. You see it was a Thursday when the rector found
me. I was in a basket with three of everything packed
with me, all of the very best quality. And there was a card
which said my name was Margaret and that fifty-two
pounds would come every year to keep me—and so it did
until last Christmas."

Miss Snelston would have liked to hear more but the
school needed her.

"Can you read and write?"

Margaret thought that a foolish question.

"Yes."

Miss Snelston turned to Peter.

"And you?"

"Oh yes, of course."

There was something about the way Peter answered
that caught Miss Snelston's ear.

"What do you read?"

"What I can get. Before . . ." Peter hesitated, then said: "Before we were sent here I was reading *David Copperfield.*"

Miss Snelston held out a hand to Horatio.

"You and Margaret can sit next to each other," she told Peter. "Horatio will be in the next room with the little ones—or can you read too, Horatio?"

Horatio shook his head.

"But I can draw pictures."

"Good," said Miss Snelston, longing to give him a hug. "If you draw a good picture we will put it up on the wall."

Back at the orphanage, Lavinia had been sent to what was called the linen room. There on a trestle table were piles of print dresses, aprons and caps made in sewing time by what Miss Jones described as "the female orphans." She held a dress up against Lavinia.

"Mostly these fit anyone," she said. "The apron ties them in."

Lavinia turned the dresses over. "There are so many pretty prints in the shops," she thought. "I wonder why they have to choose such ugly ones."

"I think I'll just take two dresses," she said. "They'll do to start with and I can buy some prettier ones later on."

Miss Jones jumped as if she had been stung by a snake.

"Prettier! Prettier! Who do you think you are! Pretty indeed! It is not prettiness that her ladyship is expecting from her scullery maid."

But Lavinia was not easily cowed.

"Did you never hear the proverb, 'He who pays the piper calls the tune'? Just now I am paying the piper and

I say I only want two print frocks. I have a black dress and coat which will do for Sundays, but I will take four aprons and caps."

Miss Jones could have shaken her. It was, she thought, foolish of Matron to have told Lavinia she had to pay for the dresses. Better to have fitted her out and then sent the bill to Lady Corkberry's housekeeper for payment to be deducted from her wages.

"Very well," she snapped. "Take what you want and then follow me. I will show you where you can sew."

The orphans came home at twelve for their dinner. This was the big meal of the day. A regular amount of food was allowed for each orphan each week and from this ration Matron was supposed to select the meals. But Matron was fond of her food so she made a point of never weighing the meat the butcher sent or the fish from the poulterer's, well knowing she would be rewarded by tasty steaks and delicate soles. As a result the main meal, though eaten to the last lick, usually left the orphans hungry.

That day the meal was a stew which should have contained at least a quarter of a pound of meat per child, but in fact was mostly turnips, parsnips and potatoes, with fragments of meat floating around. However, there had been complaints that the children went back to school hungry, so the stew was followed by a slice of suet pudding served with a teaspoonful of treacle. The suet puddings were so solid it was said if you threw one against the wall it would not break up but would bounce back to the thrower.

Margaret and Lavinia succeeded in sitting next to each other and in exchanging a little conversation.

"The school's nice," Margaret whispered. "Miss Snelston turned up Horry's suit. Nobody can read as well as Peter. We are made to point to each word as we read it."

"I'm going tomorrow," Lavinia told Margaret. "My trunk is coming this afternoon and there are things in it I want to tell you about. I'll have to wait until everybody is asleep, but I'll come and talk to you tonight."

Afternoon school was given up to the lighter subjects. First there was dancing, which Margaret loved, then there was two-part singing and finally drawing. "If only it was all school and we never had to go to the orphanage, wouldn't it be lovely?" Margaret thought, but soon school was over and Miss Jones was outside shouting "Get into line. One two. One two. No talking." Sadly, out of the corners of their eyes, the orphans watched the village children laughing and pushing each other about as they ran home to their teas.

For the orphans work was not over for the day. After tea, which was a slice of bread and margarine and a cup of milk and water, there were "tasks." Some of the girls were sent to sew, others to the kitchen to peel potatoes. For the boys there was wood to cut and bring in and what was called "repairs," which meant mending any piece of furniture which needed it.

The youngest children, of whom Horatio was one, were turned loose during this time to play. There were no toys in the so-called playroom, but the children managed without them. Almost at once Horatio was seized by two small girls who told him he was their little boy for they were going to play "Home." "Home" was an immensely popular game with the smaller children, who could spend hours pretending they were mothers and fathers—creatures few of them had seen.

Because it was an unpopular task, Margaret was sent by Miss Jones to the scullery to peel potatoes. This was supposed to be done in silence, but the cook and her assistant were out so only Winifred was in charge, and of course nobody paid any attention to her. Occasionally she squeaked:

"Oh, be quiet, do. If Matron was to hear she wouldn't half scold me." But mostly she kept darting to the scullery door to hear what was going on, for she was only thirteen and, before Matron took her on to work in the kitchen, had lived as the other orphans did.

Margaret was holding the floor. Apart from the fact that she was new so no one knew her story, she loved an audience and knew how to keep it amused. Of course she told the story of her arrival in a basket, but on this occasion she added a few touches.

"And every one of my baby clothes was embroidered with—what do you think?" It was clear the little girls couldn't think. "A coronet. And amongst my baby clothes was a beautiful diamond brooch."

Susan was among the potato peelers.

"Oh, Margaret, you are a fibber!"

"I am not," said Margaret. "I'll write to the rector to tell you it's true. Then you'll see."

"Who do you think you might be, then?" another child asked.

Margaret had so often wondered about this she had dozens of suggestions to offer.

"Well . . ." she said, "I might be . . ." From that night onward Margaret was established as the queen of storytellers.

Margaret was almost asleep by the time Lavinia felt it
safe to come to her bed. She brought with her two books,
David Copperfield and *A Tale of Two Cities.*

"These are Peter's. I can't give them to him as I can't
get into the boys' dormitory. Anyhow, I don't believe
he'd know how to hide them. Could you?"

"I can try. I put my tin box into my bed this morning
and nobody noticed, but I don't know if they look sometimes. I really ought to get them to school—they would
be safe in Peter's desk."

"Well, do what you can." Lavinia put the books on
Margaret's bed. "He must have something to read. He'd
rather read than eat. And here," she put a piece of paper
into Margaret's hand, "is my address. If anything goes
really wrong get a message to me there. Perhaps that Miss
Snelston would help—she sounds nice."

Margaret rummaged around and found her tin box
and opened it.

"I'll keep it in here. I may take this to school. I'll see.
It depends if they search our beds."

Lavinia found and held Margaret's hands.

"Don't run away, will you? It's awful enough going off
and leaving Peter and Horry, but if you weren't here I
think I'd die."

"I won't run away without telling you, I promise. But
you will come every other Sunday? Promise."

Lavinia kissed her.

"I promise, or at least, if they won't give me every
other Sunday, I'll find another place to work. I can promise you that."

"Good," said Margaret. She lay down again and, hugging her box to her, was soon asleep.

Lavinia

Lavinia drove away the next morning in an estate cart belonging to the Corkberrys. The children did not see her go as they were at school. The young man who drove the cart shouldered her tin box and, though Miss Jones saw her drive away, she neither waved nor smiled. It was a dismal departure.

Lavinia tried hard not to cry but she had to gaze out over the fields so the driver would not see that her eyes were brimming with tears. But if he could not see the young man guessed.

"Don't 'ee take on now," he said. "You'll like it up to Sedgecombe Place. They be good employers, his lordship and her ladyship. And the grub's good—far better than you would get in that old orphanage. Cruel hard on the little 'uns, they say."

The driver told Lavinia his name was Jem and that he worked with the horses. He was a cheerful youth and made Lavinia feel better.

"Do you think I shall see Lady Corkberry today?"

Jem shook his head.

"No—not her. There be a Mrs. Tanner, she be the one you'll see. She be the housekeeper. Bit of a dragon seemingly, but they say if you do your work right she'm fair."

Lavinia's heart sank. Would Mrs. Tanner want to see if she worked well before she promised her every other Sunday?

"Is it far from Sedgecombe Place—I mean from the orphanage? You see, I want to get back there on my time off. I've two little brothers there."

"Not far," said Jem, "maybe four miles—not more. Walk it easy—pretty walk too all along the canal bank."

Lavinia looked around.

"I don't see a canal."

"Not from here," Jem agreed, "but this is canal country. It's near here where the Shropshire Union Canal runs into the Staffordshire and Worcestershire Canal. I did ought to know for I was born on a canal boat."

"Were you? What made you leave it to work at Sedgecombe Place?"

"The pneumonia," Jem explained. "Cruel sick I was and down at a place called Autherley my dad had to call the doctor. Well, there wasn't no hospital near so the doctor told her ladyship about me and she fixed it so I was put to bed in the house. Well, when I was better the doctor said I wasn't to go back on the canal no more, so that's how I come to work with the horses. I see me dad and mum often enough when they're passin'. All the way to London my dad does."

Lavinia knew nothing about canals. She thought it very odd to be born on a boat.

"Have you got a lot of brothers and sisters?"

"Five. Tight squeeze it was when we was all there, but now my eldest brother he has his own boat and the next he give up same as me, then me two sisters got married so now there's only young Tom left, eleven he is, he leads the horse—not the same one, of course, but the one they give you at the stables."

"Doesn't Tom have to go to school?" Lavinia asked.

"No—canal people don't go to school. I can make me mark because one of the men I work with showed me. Young Tom would have gone to school if he could have been spared, but a course 'e couldn't be, not with there bein' nobody else for the 'orse. He don't like the canal life, Tom don't. Dad's dead scared he'll run off some-time."

"I must get someone to show me the canal path," said Lavinia. "It will be nice walking by the water now that spring's coming."

"You'll see me around," Jem promised, "and if you tell me when you have time off I'll put you on your way."

At the next bend in the road they could see Sedge-combe Place—a gray battlemented building lying in a great park.

"My word!" said Lavinia. "It is a big place. There must be a lot of servants needed to keep it right."

Jem whipped up the horse.

"You've said it." He did not speak again until he drove the cart through some wrought-iron gates. "We go up this path here, it leads to the back door."

Just as Jem had predicted, Lavinia was taken at once to be interviewed by Mrs. Tanner. She was a tall rather severe-looking woman in a black dress with a black silk apron over it. Round her waist was a chain on which hung a bunch of keys. The housekeeper's room in which she saw Lavinia was cozy, with pretty curtains and primroses in a vase. Perhaps, Lavinia thought, she is gentler than she looks. Mrs. Tanner sat upright in a stiff chair while Lavinia stood just inside the door.

"You are Lavinia Beresford?"

Lavinia curtsied.

"Yes, ma'am."

"Have you worked in a kitchen before?"

"No, ma'am. This is my first place."

Mrs. Tanner looked thoughtfully at Lavinia.

"I see. This is a big place and we all have to work hard. You will receive five pounds a year less what you have had advanced for your uniform. You will share a room with the under kitchen-maid. Between you there will be your room to do and you have to look after the rooms of three footmen. You will rise at six for, as Mrs. Smedley the cook will explain, you will have the kitchen range to see to so that the water is hot by the time she comes down. Otherwise your work is to wait on her and, of course, wash up. At night, before you go to bed, there will be the range and the kitchen and scullery to clean. At all times you will call Mrs. Smedley 'ma'am.' That is all. Do your duty and you should be very happy with us."

Lavinia could see that she was meant to curtsy and say "Thank you," but she had to arrange about her days off.

"Please, ma'am," she said, "what about my time off?"

Mrs. Tanner frowned.

"Her ladyship does not give time off to you young girls, but sometimes, if there are no guests, you may go out together in the afternoon providing you do not leave the grounds."

Lavinia swallowed nervously.

"I quite understand, ma'am, but you see I have two lit-tle brothers at the orphanage. The younger is only six. So I can only take a place where I am permitted to visit them. I had thought perhaps every other Sunday."

As she told Lady Corkberry later, Mrs. Tanner was so surprised she did not know how to answer.

"A personable young woman, m'lady, very nicely spo-ken. I did not know what to answer because I understand she wants to keep an eye on the brothers. Still, it wasn't for me to go against your rules so I said I would speak to you."

Lady Corkberry was a good woman. Taking Jem into her house when he had pneumonia was not an isolated kindness. She expected to serve her fellow-men when the opportunity offered; that, in her opinion, was what great positions and possessions were for. It was not her custom to meet her junior maids for she left their care to those immediately in charge of them, but this was an excep-tional case.

"Very well, Tanner, I will see the young woman in the morning room after breakfast tomorrow."

Lavinia found that after she had unpacked and changed she was expected to work, but not before she had eaten. Midday dinner was over in the servants' hall, but there was plenty of food about. Mrs. Smedley, a large red-faced woman, pointed to a table by the window.

"Sit there." She nodded at a dark-haired anxious-looking girl. "This is Clara. You share her room. Give her some dinner, Clara."

Lavinia remembered her instructions.

"Thank you, ma'am." She sat while Clara put in front

of her a huge plate of cold meat with a large potato in its
jacket, a jar of pickles, a loaf of bread, at least a pound of
butter and a great hunk of cheese.

"Eat up, girl," said Mrs. Smedley. "You'll find you
need to keep your strength up here."

After the food she had eaten at the orphanage Lavinia
needed no encouragement.

"My goodness," she thought, "if all the meals are like
this it will be a great temptation to take some leavings in
my pocket for the boys."

Mrs. Smedley was right about Lavinia's needing to
keep her strength up for she did find herself very tired
before she stumbled up behind Clara to their attic.
There had been guests for dinner, and after running to
and fro waiting on Mrs. Smedley all evening there had
been a great mound of washing-up to do in the scullery.
Then, after a supper taken standing up, the girls set to at
their housework.

"Terrible, isn't it?" Clara groaned. "And we've been
one short until you came. Sometimes I've been that tired
I haven't known how to get up the stairs."

But in spite of going to bed late and rising early, Lavinia looked, Lady Corkberry thought, remarkably fresh
and pretty when Mrs. Tanner brought her to her the
next morning.

"The young person Beresford, m'lady," Mrs. Tanner
said, giving a curtsy.

It was clear that Mrs. Tanner wanted to stay, but Lady
Corkberry did not permit that.

"Thank you, Tanner. You may leave us. Your name is
Lavinia Beresford?" she asked.

Lavinia curtsied.

"Yes, m'lady."

"And you have two brothers in the orphanage?"

"Yes, m'lady. Which is why I asked if I could have time off every other Sunday. I must see that they are all right."

Several things were puzzling Lady Corkberry.

"You speak very nicely. Where were you at school?"

Pain showed on Lavinia's face.

"We did lessons at home with my mother."

Lady Corkberry looked sympathetic.

"She taught you well. A pretty speaking voice is a great advantage." She hesitated. "You say you must see that your brothers are all right. Surely you know they are all right at the orphanage. It is highly spoken of."

Lavinia did not know how to answer. She did not want Lady Corkberry descending on the place for Matron would, of course, guess who had talked, which might make things harder for the boys. So she hedged.

"It's not what they are used to. It will be better when they settle down."

Lady Corkberry could feel that Lavinia was hiding something, but she did not want to bully the child.

"Very well," she said. "Every other Sunday." Then she smiled. "Perhaps one day in the summer I might have the little boys here for a treat. You would like that?"

A flush spread over Lavinia's face.

"Oh, I would, m'lady. It will be something for them to look forward to."

"Very well. Now go back to your work. I will see what can be arranged."

A Letter

Because she enjoyed the school and truly was getting to love both Miss Snelston and Polly Jenkin, Margaret, though she still meant to run away, had no immediate plans to do so. This was not only because of her promise to Lavinia and the fact that she was growing fond of Peter and Horry, but also because of her Sunday underclothes. Whenever she thought of that lace-edged petticoat and those drawers she was so full of rage she felt she could not run away until in some way she had paid Matron back. Poor Susan, on the walk to school, would have been bored to exhaustion with the subject of the lace on Margaret's Sunday underclothes only Margaret was always inventing new things she would like to do to Matron and Susan enjoyed hearing about those.

"I would like a great enormous saucepan full of frying fat," Margaret would whisper through the hood of her cape, "and I'd push her in and fry her and fry her until she was dead." Or, on another day: "I thought of something in bed last night. I would shut her up in a cupboard with thousands and thousands of hungry rats so they would eat every bit of her."

But Margaret did not only plan horrible ends for Matron. She collected information about her from the children, particularly those who had been in the orphanage since they were babies. As a result, she gradually built up a picture of the way Matron managed things. She learned that in May each year Matron had a holiday. She went up north, it was said, to visit a brother, and that was when—so the story went—she sold any clothes belonging to new orphans which were worth selling.

"She goes away with a great big box," a child called Chloe told Margaret, "and it weighs ever such a lot because Mr. Toms has to carry it"—Mr. Toms was the beadle—"and he swears ever so, but when she comes back it's so light anyone could carry it."

"Clothes wouldn't weigh all that lot," said Margaret.

"It's not only clothes," Chloe whispered, "it's food. Our food. Last year we nearly starved before she went so she could take a huge joint of beef to her brother, and sausages and pounds and pounds of cheese."

"How do you know?" Margaret asked.

"Winifred, of course. They think because she works in the kitchen she's one of them, but she never is, she's still one of us."

Margaret, turning over these scraps of information in her head, saw that they made a pattern. Somehow, before

Matron went away in May, she must get back the clothes Hannah had made for her. And somehow she must get hold of her jersey and skirt before she ran away.

Meanwhile, Margaret did what she could to look after Peter and Horry, often getting punished for it. Punishments in the orphanage were tough. They ranged from being sent to bed without supper to beatings. In between there were other terrors, such as being locked in a cupboard, being tied to a tree in the garden or being shamed by being sent to church on Sundays without a white fichu or, in the case of the boys, a white collar; this told the whole congregation a child was in disgrace. By suggestion, the children had learned to look upon being disgraced in church as the worst punishment of all.

The very morning Lavinia left, Margaret had secreted Peter's two books under her cape and carried them to school. At school she had put them in his desk.

"You can read all through playtime," she told him, "and other times perhaps if you ask Miss Snelston."

Peter was delighted to see his books again, but he absolutely refused to keep both in his desk.

"I must have a book in the orphanage, Margaret. It's awful as it is, but with no book I think I'd die."

"But when could you read?" Margaret asked him. "I know we are supposed to have free time every day, but mostly we don't."

"It's better for us boys, I think," Peter explained. "At least that's what the boys say. They say Mr. Toms doesn't seem to mind if they don't do much as long as Matron doesn't know. They say he hates Matron."

"I bet he does. Who wouldn't!" Margaret agreed. "But where will you keep a book?"

"I'll find a place," said Peter confidently. "Out-of-doors somewhere, but of course safe from rain."

Margaret looked in surprise at Peter. He was such a thin, pale little boy. Most of his face seemed to be eyes. Yet he wasn't at all weak, at least he wasn't about things he cared about—like books. She had been thinking of him as a small boy, but now she remembered he was as old as she was.

"Will you take a book home tonight?"

"Of course," said Peter calmly. "Those horrible cloaks aren't good for anything except hiding things in."

But in spite of Peter's confidence, Margaret felt responsible for him, so after tea she nipped out before tasks to see where the book was to be hidden. Peter had been ordered to act as donkey to the big lawn mower, tugging it along by ropes worn over each shoulder while another boy pushed. This suited Peter perfectly.

"This is grand," he told Margaret. "Harry"—he indicated the other boy—"says it's all right if I read while I'm doing it. He'll shout if I go crooked."

That was the first time Margaret was caught and punished. She was slipping back into the orphanage when she ran slap into Miss Jones, who turned puce with rage.

"Margaret Thursday! Where have you been? I distinctly heard Matron say you were to help in the kitchen."

Margaret thought quickly. Whatever happened she must not mention Peter.

"I thought I heard a cat crying."

"A cat!" Miss Jones's face turned even more puce. "We have no cats here. With a hundred orphans to feed and clothe we cannot afford to keep a cat."

"Thank goodness!" thought Margaret. "Poor cat, it

would starve in this place." Out loud she said: "May I go to the kitchen?"

"At once," Miss Jones ordered. "But this will, of course, be reported to Matron and you will be punished."

"I think that's mean when I was only trying to help a cat that wasn't there," said Margaret, and dashed off to the kitchen.

Miss Jones, on her way to Matron's office, muttered: "That is a very unpleasant child. There is something impertinent about her."

Matron, when told about Margaret and the supposed cat, agreed with Miss Jones about the unpleasantness of Margaret.

"One of these independent children," she agreed. "It will take time before she is molded to our shape. Send her to me when she comes in from school tomorrow. She shall have ten strokes on each hand. That will teach her who is the ruler in this establishment."

It was very difficult to help Horatio, but he so badly needed help Margaret did all that she could. There were two periods when he needed her most. One was morning washing time and the other was his free time when he came home from school. Two ex-orphans not suitable for farm work were employed on the boys' side of the home to help keep discipline and to wash the little boys. They were loutish types in their late teens who enjoyed their small power and showed it by bullying and taking pleasure in being rough. It made Margaret mad to see poor Horry come into the diningroom, his eyes red from soap, his cheeks shiny from tears. But Margaret, though seething with rage, kept her temper. She could do nothing for the time being for it was past imagining what the punishment would be if a girl was found in the boys' dormitory.

"Most likely I'd be beaten so hard I'd die," she thought, "and that wouldn't help Horry."

Then she had an idea. When she had opened her wicker basket on the train to give everybody toffee, she had told Lavinia she had three stamps. Lavinia already had a pretty shrewd idea what the orphanage was going to be like.

"Hide them," she advised. "Stick them inside one of your boots. They won't find them there."

So far Margaret had not used a stamp for she did not want to write to Hannah or the rector with news which must depress them, for what could they do? And she certainly was not going to tell Hannah what had happened to her underclothes. But that meant she still had her three stamps and one of these she used to write to Lavinia. She took off the boot in which the stamps were stuck to the inside of the toe and took one out. Miss Snelston gave her a piece of lined paper and an envelope and promised to post the letter.

Margaret had never received a letter. Although she did not know it, she would have been receiving letters regularly from the rector had not the archdeacon warned him that it had been found letters upset the orphans and so they were discouraged. Margaret was very hazy as to how a letter should be worded. However, she did her best and at least got over what she wanted to say. She wrote:

"Margaret Thursday says when you come on Sunday she would be obliged if you could bring some sweets to bribe that beast Ben who washes Horatio very faithfully Margaret Thursday."

Plans for Sunday

Quite by chance, Margaret learned where Matron kept the orphans' own clothes. It was through a girl at school called Sally. Her father had met with an accident and as a result could only do part-time work, so Sally's mother helped out taking any little job she could get. One morning Sally said to Margaret:

"My ma is goin' up to your old orphanage next week."

"What for?" Margaret asked.

"It's work she does for the matron—dead scared of your matron my ma is."

"I don't wonder," said Margaret. "I think 'most everybody is."

"It's washin' and mendin' she does," Sally explained.

Margaret was amazed.

"Washing! I can't think why Matron pays your mother to do that for us female orphans do it all day Saturdays. Cruelly hard it is, especially the ironing. You try washing

for one hundred orphans. The senior girls have to do
Matron's caps as well, and all the week at 'tasks' some of
us mend.''

"It's not what you wear my ma does,'' Sally explained.
"It's special stuff. Kept locked up at the top of the house,
my ma says. When it's done my ma has to pack it ready to
travel when your matron goes on her holiday.''

Sally had moved away so she did not see how Margaret's eyes flashed and her chin shot into the air. Getting
Sally's mother to pack the clothes Hannah had made for
her, was she! Mean beast! But Margaret kept her head.
Nobody—nobody at all must guess what she planned.
Think as she would, though, she could not imagine what
she would do with her lace-edged petticoat and drawers
when she got them. She just knew that somehow she must
get them back. Hannah's lovely present was not going up
north for Matron to sell.

Although she was a very busy person, Lady Corkberry
had not forgotten her nicely-spoken scullery maid. In the
week before Lavinia's first half-day she spoke about her
to the housekeeper when she came for orders.

"Good morning, Tanner. Before I forget, that new
scullery maid, Lavinia Beresford, is to be allowed to visit
her brothers in the orphanage this coming Sunday. She
must be home before dark so she may leave immediately
after church. Will you see that a generous lunch is
packed with some sweet cakes which she will no doubt
wish to share with the little boys.''

Mrs. Tanner was very fond of her mistress and used to
her ways. She thought it amazing that a great lady should
remember the half-day of a new scullery maid, but she

was like that. So she made a note on her pad. Then she had an idea.

"I was hearing there is something for us at the station at Wolverhampton, m'lady—garden stuff, I believe. It wouldn't be much farther for the cart to go on to the orphanage to tell them the girl will be coming on Sunday. It would be a pity if her brothers were out."

"What a capital idea!" said Lady Corkberry. "Will you see to it?"

"Of course, m'lady," Mrs. Tanner agreed.

That was the day when Margaret's letter for Lavinia arrived. She read it, amused at its formality, but worried by its contents. She had no money to buy sweets and she did not know when she would be paid the balance of the five pounds a year. Over washing-up, she asked advice of her roommate, Clara.

Clara, as usual, looked worried.

"I wish I could help, but my mother has all my money; sometimes she gives me a tanner for myself, but I haven't got anything now and won't have till old mother Smedley gives me my penny for the plate on Sunday."

Each Sunday before the staff left for church the heads of departments saw that their juniors were properly dressed, had clean handkerchiefs and money for the plate.

"My penny for the plate!" said Lavinia. "That would buy sweets."

Clara, who was drying, nearly dropped a bowl.

"Lavinia Beresford! You wouldn't dare take money from the church. Why, you might be struck dead."

Lavinia laughed.

"I wouldn't be, you know. Jesus loved children and he

wouldn't grudge me keeping my penny if it was to help Horatio."

"Don't do it," Clara implored. "Even if you aren't struck dead, Mrs. Smedley or someone might see, which would be almost as bad."

Lavinia laughed again, but what Clara had said gave her an idea.

"All right, I won't take my church penny. I'll tell Mrs. Smedley why I want it and ask her for a little advance."

Lavinia got her chance to speak to Mrs. Smedley when that lady came down from her room for afternoon tea. Although the cakes and scones for the drawing room were made in the kitchen, Mrs. Smedley had nothing to do with the actual meal, for food such as scones was collected from the under-cook by one of the footmen, and the cakes were arranged and sandwiches were cut by the butler who, with the footmen, served the tea. So about five o'clock Mrs. Smedley, refreshed by a good sleep, could come down to a kitchen scrubbed and cleaned by her juniors, to find her tea waiting on the table.

Kitchen tea was far more substantial than drawing-room tea. There was always a tasty dish of some sort as well as dripping toast and large slices of rich fruit cake. This meal was eaten by all the kitchen staff, for usually there was a busy night ahead with at least six courses to be served for dinner, so there was no time for them to eat until quite late.

Tea over, Mrs. Smedley would change from the cheerful woman who had come down for her tea into a fury. Not that she felt like a fury, but she considered that it was part of her role to let everybody know who was who so far as the kitchen was concerned. So the moment tea was cleared away she was giving out her orders with the rapidity of a machine gun. But though she was very much the general commanding the battle when there was dinner to be cooked, she never really lost her warm heart. For whenever there were guests, which meant extra hard work for everybody, she would open the cooking sherry and pour out for each of her staff a good glassful and see that they drank it.

"Now, no faces," she would say to the girls who hated sherry. "Drink it up. It's a tonic and you'll need it before the night is out."

That day Lavinia caught Mrs. Smedley at her tea. She was beaming and rosy fresh from her sleep and enjoying a couple of juicy kippers.

"Well, dear," she asked, "what can I do for you?"

Lavinia, seeing how good-humored Mrs. Smedley looked, decided to take her into her confidence as far as she could—that is to say, without actually complaining of the orphanage. For she knew Mrs. Smedley was the sort of woman who, if she suspected cruelty, would dash straight to Mrs. Tanner demanding that someone visit the orphanage immediately. And how would that help poor Peter and Horry?

"It's a note I had from a girl at the orphanage, ma'am. She asked me if, when I go on Sunday, I could bring some sweets. You see, my little brother Horatio is only six and he needs a bit of help at washing and dressing, and this girl thought it would help if I brought some sweets that could be handed out as a sort of thank-you to those who help him."

Mrs. Smedley looked up from her kipper and her

shrewd eyes studied Lavinia.

"There's stories told about that orphanage. Are they true?"

Lavinia hesitated.

"I was there only one night. It was all right as far as I could see."

Mrs. Smedley went back to her kippers.

"Each Saturday before your Sunday off remind me you're going. I'll see there's a nice basket to take with you so you can have a picnic. Now, about these sweets. You want some money, I suppose? Remind me tomorrow when I've got my purse. You can have a shilling."

At exactly this time back at the orphanage Jem was pulling up the horse who pulled the cart outside the entrance. He hitched the reins over a paling and ran up the steps. Miss Jones answered the bell.

"Yes?" she said.

Jem handed her an envelope.

"It's from Sedgecombe Place."

"I suppose that girl we sent is giving trouble," Miss Jones thought. Out loud she said: "Wait here. I will see if there is an answer."

Matron was in her office. She cut open the stiff envelope and drew out a sheet of crested paper. The letter was from Mrs. Tanner.

"I am asked to inform you that on this Sunday next Lavinia Beresford will visit the orphanage in the afternoon for the purpose of seeing her brothers. Her ladyship would be obliged if the little boys could be waiting for her and some place found where they can be by themselves. A. Tanner (Housekeeper)."

But Mrs. Tanner had talked to Lavinia before she sent the letter so there was a postscript. "Her ladyship would be glad if you would also allow Margaret Thursday to see Lavinia as she has shown kindness to the two little boys."

Matron muttered: "Tell him the children will be waiting," which sent Miss Jones scurrying back to Jem. Alone, she looked at the letter as if she could have bitten it. "Her ladyship would be obliged if the little boys could be waiting." The nerve of it! She didn't want that Lavinia coming back here. Carrying tales she'd be, as like as not. And why Margaret Thursday? What kindness had she ever shown Peter or Horatio? It was a sneaking, low-down way of getting the orphanage talked about, that's what it was. But if there was talk she'd know where it started and she'd have the hide off Margaret Thursday if it was the last thing she did.

Half a Sunday

Sunday was a lovely day. All the household at Sedge-combe Place got up an hour later than usual, so Clara and Lavinia did not have to be down until seven. Lavinia, when she woke, ran straight to the window and looked out.

"Oh, Clara! The sky's as blue as blue and that field over there is gold with buttercups."

Clara came yawning to the window.

"I'm glad it's fine for you, but you wouldn't catch me walking all that way on me half-day. I always say to me mum when I get home all I want is to put me feet up."

Clara's mother had been in service in Sedgecombe Place and had married one of the under-gardeners. They lived in a cottage on the estate, so Clara was allowed home most Sundays.

"Does your mother let you put your feet up?" Lavinia asked.

Clara gave Lavinia a friendly dig with her elbow.

"Give over! Is it likely with ten little 'uns to look after? Why, I'm not inside the door before it's 'Clara do this,' 'Clara do that.' "

Lavinia leaned against the window.

"I do wish I had something pretty to wear to match the weather. It's not a day for black."

It was a rule of the house that all the servants wore black for church on Sundays.

"Can't you change?" Clara suggested.

"No, I was told specially I could leave right after church."

"Tell you what," Clara suggested. "When 'they' "—"they" was how the staff usually referred to the family—"have gone, take off your hat and give it to me. Proper figure of fun we look in them."

All the women servants had to wear small black hats to church or else black bonnets. The hats, which were provided, were made of unbendable chipped straw with a band of narrow ribbon around them. It was said in the servants' hall that they were chosen because they were guaranteed to suit nobody.

Lavinia poured some cold water from a jug into a tin basin and started to wash.

"What a good idea! I was going to put it in my basket with my lunch, but if you'll take it home it'll be lots better. I'll let my hair loose. I hate it up."

As the village church was not far away the staff walked to matins through the grounds on fine Sundays. When it was wet they were driven in a carriage. That Sunday Lavinia, walking last as became her humble position, almost danced down the drive. She was carrying the basket Mrs. Smedley had given her. It was quite heavy so she was sure it was full of good things. On top of it she had put the bag of sweets, chosen with care to prove irresistible to the Ben who washed Horry. Suddenly she heard a whistle and there was Jem looking around a rhododendron bush. Lavinia, on an afternoon walk in the grounds, had told him this was her Sunday to visit the orphanage, but he had not known then how much free time he would have. Now he had good news.

"I got the half-day too, see, so I can walk most of the way with you. I'll wait on the canal bank—I'd like a word with them on the canal boats on account they may have seen my dad, see? Then I can take you home."

Lavinia was delighted.

"Could you really! I would like that. I have to be back at the house before dark, but it's a long walk and I'd enjoy your company."

Jem thought this very fancy talk so all he said was:

"See you after church," and disappeared back behind the rhododendron.

Every weekday at Sedgecombe Place there were family prayers. These were led by Lord Corkberry and all the staff had to attend in strict order of precedence, starting with the butler and finishing with Lavinia. Sunday morning service was, Lavinia thought, very like family prayers, for again the staff lined up behind the butler and sat in pews in strict precedence, again finishing with herself. That Sunday she was glad that she came last because it gave her a chance to hand the verger her precious basket and ask him to look after it.

It was peaceful in the little church, with the smell of wallflowers blowing in through the door and doves cooing on the roof. Ordinarily Lavinia would have enjoyed the service, glad of the chance to sit down and join in singing favorite hymns to well-known tunes. But that day she could not get her mind off Peter and Horry. Had they been told yet that she was coming? And would she be allowed to see Margaret?

After church all the staff had to form up in two lines on either side of the churchyard path. Then, as Lord and Lady Corkberry and any guests they might have passed, all the men had to raise their hats and the women curtsied. Usually the Corkberrys would nod and smile in reply, though sometimes they would pause to speak. That morning Lady Corkberry stopped in front of Lavinia.

"Have they given you a good packed lunch?"

Lavinia gave another curtsy.

"Oh yes, m'lady. I haven't looked but it feels heavy."

Lord Corkberry was a man who liked to spend his life on a horse, though he would sometimes shoot game or go fishing. He left the running of his house entirely to his wife and seldom spoke to the indoor servants. Now, to Lady Corkberry's surprise, he spoke to Lavinia.

"And where have you secreted this packed lunch which you have not seen but which feels heavy?"

Poor Lavinia, with all the servants' eyes on her, turned pink. She gave yet another curtsy.

"I—I asked the verger to look after it, m'lord."

Lady Corkberry smiled.

"Have a pleasant day." Then she moved on.

When they were out of earshot, Lord Corkberry asked his wife:

"Who is that girl, Rose?"

Lady Corkberry was surprised at his interest.

"The new scullery maid. She has two little brothers at the orphanage whom she is going to visit."

"Funny," said Lord Corkberry, "she's the dead spittin' image of somebody. Can't remember who, but it will come back."

The Corkberrys and the heads of staff out of sight, Lavinia dashed into the church to retrieve her basket, tossed her despised hat to Clara, and joined Jem at the church gate.

At all times a canal bank is a fascinating place. That morning in April it seemed to Lavinia to have magic about it. There were primroses and cuckoo flowers along the banks, and in the woods she could see celandines and wood anemones. Jem could not understand her excitement.

"They'm pretty all right, but you don't have time for no prettiness when you have to lead the horse what pulls the boat. Very contrary critters canal 'orses can be."

Lavinia forced herself to attend to Jem.

"Fancy being born on a boat. It must have been odd."

"Not really. It's what you're used to, I suppose, but it was a tight squeeze. Our boat, *The Crusader* she's called, like all canal boats is only seven feet. There's two cabins, one fore and one aft, with a cross-bed for Dad and Mum. Well, you can see with six of us there wasn't much room for larkin' or that."

Lavinia looked at the canal, so quiet with trees reflected on it, while a mother moorhen taught her babies their way around, and a heron flashed low over the water looking for a fish.

"I wonder why you and your brothers hated the canal life. It looks fun to me. I'd love to walk along leading a horse."

Jem sniffed.

"Think you'd love it, do you? That's all you know. You try it all weathers. Mind you, though it's cruel 'ard on the boys it's worse on the 'orses. There's stables all up and down the canal and we 'ires them from there. A canal boat loaded weighs maybe twenty, maybe thirty ton and the 'orse has to pull that weight eighteen maybe twenty hour a day, and when he has to start the boat movin' it's wicked for there's the weight of the water added."

"Poor horses!" Lavinia agreed, but her mind was only half with Jem. The weather was lovely and soon she would see the boys.

Jem left Lavinia about a mile from the orphanage.

"I shall wait here," he said. "Should be a boat along any time now. See you later."

"Dear Jem, thank you so much," said Lavinia, and hurried off along the path.

The Picnic

Matron did not mention to Margaret, Peter or Horatio that Lavinia was coming until after midday dinner. Sunday dinner was the big meal of the week so was enormously looked forward to by the orphans. Sometimes it was boiled silverside with dumplings and on another Sunday roast beef with Yorkshire pudding. Actually, whatever was served, there were more of the dumplings or pudding on each plate than meat, but the orphans didn't mind—suet or pudding made you feel full and that was something they seldom felt.

After grace had been sung, Matron held up a hand for silence.

"Seeing the day is so fine you may all take your prayer books into the garden for an hour and learn the collect for the day outside. I shall hear you repeat this myself this evening. You little ones who cannot read can look at the Bible picture books. When the hour is up, Miss Jones will give you all Sunday tasks, during which you will take turns to read out loud *Pilgrim's Progress*. I wish to speak to Peter and Horatio Beresford and Margaret Thursday."

All day Margaret had been waiting for a message. This was Lavinia's half-Sunday. She didn't suppose she would be allowed to see her, but she meant to have a good try, and anyway Lavinia would bring sweets for that awful Ben.

Matron waited until the orphans had filed out, then she ordered Peter, Horatio and Margaret to stand in front of her. She fixed her eyes on Peter.

"I have received a letter from Sedgecombe Place. Your sister Lavinia is being allowed to visit you this afternoon. As an exception I am allowing her to take you and Horatio for a walk."

Nobody ever went outside the orphanage except to school or church. Even Peter, vague as he was, knew this. A walk with Lavinia! It was a glorious promise. His eyes shone.

"Oh, thank you, Matron."

Matron turned to Margaret.

"Lady Corkberry is under the illusion that you have been of service to Peter and Horatio so she asks that you may be allowed to join the party. I was much inclined to refuse this request for I am far from satisfied with your behavior, but as the suggestion comes from Lady Corkberry I have decided—unwillingly—to allow this great treat, so you may join the Beresford boys on their walk with Lavinia."

Margaret had to hold her tongue between her teeth to

prevent herself from answering. She longed to say: "Thank you—but I don't want any favors from you." Instead, splendidly conscious that she had arrived on the church steps with three of everything all of the very best quality, whereas Matron when a baby was most likely dressed in passed-down woolens which were gray with age, she gave a curtsy. Then, smiling sweetly, she said:

"Thank you kindly, Matron."

Matron could feel that somehow Margaret, impertinent child that she was, was making fun of her, but she could say nothing, so she strode out of the dining room, calling over her shoulder:

"Get ready now. You can sit in the hall until Lavinia arrives."

The Sunday fichus on the girls and white collars on the boys gave the orphans a cared-for look. Nevertheless Lavinia was shocked when she saw Margaret and Peter. Horry, she noticed thankfully, was much as usual. But Peter's face had shrunk and his eyes seemed to have grown bigger. Margaret seemed to be much paler and her hair, though still curling under her cap, was less defiant. Lavinia put down her basket and knelt in the hall hugging all three to her while she murmured: "My darlings! My poor darlings!"

Margaret said: "Matron said we could go for a walk with you."

Lavinia was delighted.

"We'll have a picnic. I saw a wood not far off and I've got the food in this basket."

For a picnic the despised brown cloaks came into their own. Lavinia spread them out so there was room for everybody to sprawl on them without getting damp. As the

children had just eaten their dinners she decided to serve the meal as late as possible so they could enjoy it. "After all," she thought, "I eat well every day so it won't hurt me to have my dinner late for once."

"Vinia," Horatio demanded, "I think there's wolves in this wood. Can I go and look?"

Lavinia took off his Sunday collar.

"Of course you can, and if you find a friendly one you might bring it back with you. Give me your collar, Peter. We mustn't mess them up and you can go wolf-hunting too."

Peter obediently took off his collar.

"Did you bring me a book? I'm reading as slow as slow, but I've nearly finished *A Tale of Two Cities* and I'm over halfway through *David Copperfield*."

"Not this week I didn't, but I'll see if I can get hold of anything for next time. Aren't there any books in the orphanage?"

"Just *Pilgrim's Progress* and some Bible picture books, and they are kept in Matron's room," Margaret explained.

Lavinia, having no idea how she would manage it, repeated her promise to try to get hold of something. This seemed to satisfy Peter for he ran off with Horatio.

"Are you happy to stay here," Lavinia asked Margaret, "or would you like to pick primroses?"

Margaret stared at her, surprised that anyone so sensible could ask so silly a question.

"What could I do with primroses?"

"I suppose that even in the orphanage there must be a jam jar."

Margaret took off her fichu lest she crumple it.

"I should have thought even in the little time you were there you would know orphans don't have flowers. In fact, orphans don't have anything. I've still got that box Hannah gave me that the toffees were in. I keep it in my bed, but they'd take it away if they knew and I'd be punished."

"How do they punish you?"

Margaret held out a hand which had red marks across the palm where she had been given ten strokes with a switch.

Lavinia drew in her breath.

"Do Peter and Horry get beaten like that?"

"Neither of them have got punished yet. The things Peter does, like reading when he's pulling the mowing machine, they don't know, and the little ones get slapped rather than real punishments."

Lavinia took Margaret's hand and looked at it.

"Mean beasts!"

"Truly, I'd rather have my hands hit than some of the other punishments. I hate being locked in a cupboard and it's pretty awful being sent to bed without supper because you are so hungry you can't sleep."

"You and Peter look as if you were usually hungry— Horry doesn't look so bad."

"That is because of Polly Jenkin. She helps Miss Snelston who is head teacher. They are both awfully nice. Polly is very fond of Horatio and she sneaks things to him when the others aren't looking. Good things like sandwiches full of meat and hard-boiled eggs, and often he gets a glass of milk."

"God bless Polly!" said Lavinia. "I do hope some day I can thank her."

Margaret looked worried.

"I know Peter is getting thin, but it's difficult to help him. You see, the boys and the female orphans don't often meet. Sometimes I sneak out to talk to Peter, but if I'm caught I'm punished. But I've got a plan." She lowered her voice as if even there Matron could hear. "The cook—she's called Mrs. Bones, and it's a good name for her for all we get is bones—well, she has to cook Matron's supper. If she knew I could cook I think she'd be glad to let me do it for she says she's on her feet all day and they hurt something chronic. Well, I'm working on Winifred, who is in the kitchen, to tell Mrs. Bones about me, and if I get a chance to cook I'll get some pickings, and I'll share them with Peter and Horry. I don't care what punishments I get."

Lavinia looked fondly at Margaret.

"You are a kind girl."

"Not really," said Margaret. "Mostly it's sort of revenge. I despise Matron so much I don't care what I do to annoy her."

The picnic was a wild success. There were such delicious things in the basket. Sandwiches of all sorts, a fruit pie, cakes, biscuits and a slab of chocolate. With cries of delight, the hungry children fell on the food until there was not a crumb left. They were so busy eating they did not notice that Lavinia gave them everything, eating nothing herself.

"What's in that bag, Vinia?" Horatio demanded.

Lavinia handed the bag to Margaret.

"It's sweets. Peter is going to give one to Ben every day so that he does not put soap in your eyes."

"Where shall we hide them?" Peter asked.

"At school," said Margaret. "You can bring one back every day."

Lavinia was very silent on the walk home to Sedgecombe Place. It had made her cry to leave the children at the orphanage. Surely somewhere there was a better place that would take them in.

Jem was used to being on his own so he respected Lavinia's silence and walked on ahead whistling.

When Lavinia got in Mrs. Smedley was starting to prepare Sunday supper. She looked out of the window where the sun was setting.

"Just in time," she said. "There's a good girl. I'm giving them macaroni and cheese for a hot dish so, as my girl's out, you can grate the cheese for me." Then she noticed that Lavinia looked tired. "But have some tea first."

In the kitchen there was a cupboard called "The Housemaids' Cupboard." This was always bulging with snacks: game, cold chicken, cold meats, as well as fruit puddings and cakes. Any of the staff could help themselves from that cupboard whenever they felt hungry. Lavinia took a plate and piled on to it a rich assortment of food. Then, fetching a knife and fork, she sat down at the table by the window and ate the lot.

Mrs. Smedley watched her. She had packed the luncheon basket herself so she knew what had been in it. At last she asked: "Was the dinner all right?"

Lavinia looked up apologetically from her plate.

"Lovely. I was able to share it with the boys and Margaret."

"Share nothing," thought Mrs. Smedley. "I think you thought the children were hungry and gave them the lot. I'll have a word with Mrs. Tanner about that orphanage and maybe she'll find a way to pass it on."

A Night Adventure

By tactful questioning, Margaret managed to get some news out of Sally.

"My mum is going up to your old orphanage after dinner on Tuesday."

It was all very well to have the information, but Margaret could not imagine how she would use it. But she was determined that somehow she would. So on the Monday after the picnic she decided, as a first step, to find out where the room was in which Sally's mother would work. Sally had said "at the top of the house"—a part of the building no orphan had ever seen. Margaret, by talking to Winifred, collected a little more information.

"I sleep on top under the roof with Mary," Winifred said—Mary was Mrs. Bones's kitchen maid. "Funny little room it is, with the water tank in the corner what makes noises like an old man with the wheezes. Still, it's not so bad on account there's only us so we can do what we like up there. Mrs. Bones wouldn't half take a turn if she could see what we sneaks up for our suppers."

"Lucky you!" Margaret had said. "I'd love to sleep in the only room at the top of the house. It's awful sharing with forty-nine other girls."

"Don't I remember!" Winifred had agreed. "Sniffin' and snuffin', not to say throwin' up at times." She lowered her voice. "But it's not the only room. There's another where Matron keeps you-know-what."

Margaret kept from showing that she was bursting with interest.

"Have you ever seen inside?"

Winifred shook her head.

"Not likely!" There was drama in her voice. "I wouldn't dare go in. It wouldn't surprise me if, as well as the clothes what we know are there, there wasn't some dead orphans poked away in a cupboard."

Margaret carefully planned her time for exploring. Winifred had to carry in Matron's supper the moment the last orphan had gone upstairs to bed. Miss Jones, having put out the lights in the girls' dormitory, retired to her room, which was just off the passageway outside. She, like all the staff except Matron, had eaten her supper with the orphans. As bread, margarine and cocoa were barely enough to keep the orphans alive, it was likely that somehow Miss Jones got hold of something extra and ate it in her room. So just after lights out was the ideal time, but the snag was that just after lights out few of the orphans were asleep.

No one dared to get out of bed for fear Miss Jones would reappear, which sometimes she did, but there was a lot of whispering and giggling from bed to bed. If the orphans saw Margaret get out of bed and leave the dormitory one of them would be certain to tattletale, for talebearing was rewarded, usually with an extra slice of bread and margarine, though sometimes with a real luxury like a piece of cheese. But Margaret had it all planned. Softly as a kitten jumping, she eased herself out of bed and then lay flat on the floor; from there she rolled from bed to bed until she reached the end of the room next to the door.

Miss Jones always wedged the dormitory door open so that she could hear if there was any disturbance. There was a gas jet in the passageway, but it was turned very low so there was little light. Fortunately Violet, the child in the bed by the door, had her back to it when Margaret reached the door, for she was whispering to the girl next to her. So, still flat on the ground, Margaret was able to crawl out. But as she crawled she passed over a loose board which gave a loud creak. Had anybody heard? Violet had. She shot up, stifling a scream.

"There's a burglar outside, I'm sure there is," Margaret heard her whisper.

"What would a burglar come here for?" another girl replied. "D'you think he's after our uniforms? Or maybe he'd fancy my nightie?"

This witticism was relayed up and down the dormitory, causing explosions of laughter.

"I better move," thought Margaret. "If that noise doesn't bring old Jones nothing will."

Margaret got to her feet and ran down the corridor to the stairs. She was just going to climb them when she heard Miss Jones open her door. Quickly, she lay down flat against the banister.

From where she was she could see Miss Jones, who had

not yet undressed, go to the dormitory door.

"Who was laughing?" she asked.

In a frightened squeak, Violet answered:

"Please'm, I mean Miss Jones'm. I thought I heard a burglar."

Miss Jones expressed astonishment by using the word "burglar" like a piano. She started on a low note and rose almost an octave.

"A burglar? And what, pray, would a burglar want here?"

Violet was evidently nearly in tears.

"I don't know, Miss Jones."

Miss Jones had not come to the dormitory unarmed. Out of her pocket she took a hairbrush.

"A girl who keeps others awake must be punished," she said.

Margaret could hear no more except muffled cries. Too well she knew what was happening. Poor Violet was being beaten on her behind with a hairbrush, and very painful it was. Margaret was sorry and decided, as it was her fault, to give Violet one of Ben's sweets in school the next day. Then, taking advantage of Miss Jones's being by Violet's bed, she ran up the stairs.

The boys' dormitory was over the girls' room. Here the same system prevailed. The dormitory door was ajar, there was a low gaslight left on all night, and the room which on the floor below belonged to Miss Jones was on the boys' floor occupied by Mr. Toms, the beadle. It was orphanage gossip that he liked a glass or two of porter at night and did not expect to be disturbed unless an orphan was so ill death might be expected. Margaret, relying on this gossip being true, ran up the corridor and climbed the last flight of stairs.

There was not a sound on the top floor except the wheezing of the water tank. Margaret was not surprised at the quiet, for she knew Mary and Winifred would not be up yet. There were two doors just as Winifred had described, and she knew which was the room she wanted because behind the other door she could hear the wheezing tank. Quietly she turned the handle. To her surprise the door opened. She closed it softly behind her and looked around. There was a moon that night and by its light she could see that the room was empty except for a table, a chair and two large cupboards standing side by side just away from the wall. Margaret tugged and pulled at the doors of the cupboards, but they held firm. She was wasting her time for both were locked.

"I can't break them open," thought Margaret, "so I must get the keys or I must get up here when Sally's mother is working and pretend that Matron wants her or something."

It was no good hanging about for she had still to undergo the adventurous journey back to her bed. So she went to the door and had just opened it when she heard heavy breathing and steps climbing the stairs, preceded by the flickering light of a candle.

"Matron!" thought Margaret. Softly she closed the door. Then she dashed across the room and squeezed herself behind the cupboards.

By Moonlight

Evidently Matron, too, did not want to be seen. Margaret heard her pause outside and was certain she was making sure that Mary and Winifred had not yet finished in the kitchen. Then, just as quietly as Margaret had done, she opened the door, and equally quietly shut it behind her.

Margaret, squeezed behind the cupboards, could only guess what Matron was doing. She was so frightened she could hear her heart beating and wondered that Matron could not hear it too. "Oh, dear God," she prayed, "don't let me sneeze—please don't let me for I think if Matron finds me here she'll kill me, truly I do. I don't know how. Maybe she'il throw me out of the window and say I jumped, or lock me up forever and ever with no food."

From what she could hear, Margaret guessed that Matron was unlocking the cupboards and then taking things out and putting them on the table.

"I guess she's getting things ready for Sally's mother," thought Margaret. "Oh, I wish I could see what she's put out. I wonder if my Sunday clothes with lace on them are there."

Matron seemed to be lifting things or perhaps stretching up to the top shelves for something, for Margaret could hear some agonized squeaking from her corset bones.

After what seemed to take an hour but was really twenty minutes, Matron evidently finished what she had come to do for Margaret heard her go to the door, open it quietly then close it behind her. Then she heard another sound—a key being fitted in the lock. Then, with awful finality, it was turned!

Margaret heard the key pulled out. Then she heard the stairs creak as Matron went down them with, no doubt, the key in her pocket.

Margaret wriggled out from behind the cupboards. The moon had temporarily disappeared behind a cloud so she could see nothing. For a moment she panicked and might have flung herself against the door and screamed, but just in time she pulled herself together. "I must wait," she told herself, "until the moon comes back, then I'll see what I can do. There must be a way I can get out, there absolutely must."

A minute later the moon reappeared. It was nearly full and seemed to be shining straight in at the window. It lit up the table and now Margaret could see what Matron had been doing. On the table there was a pile of clothes, all in miserable condition, dirty and torn, evidently the clothes Sally's mother had to wash and mend. But of her own clothes and wicker basket there wasn't a sign. "I expect they're in these cupboards," Margaret thought, and turned to look at them. Her eyes widened. For some reason, perhaps because when Sally's mother had finished washing and mending the clothes they were to go back in the cupboards, Matron had left them both open. Margaret looked in one cupboard and then the other. In the second cupboard she saw her underclothes laid out on one shelf and her wicker basket on another.

It was so exciting to see the clothes again that, for a moment, it made Margaret forget the terrible position she was in. Suddenly it was as if Hannah were in the room with her. "Three of everything," Margaret heard her say. "Three plain cambric petticoats. Three pairs of drawers with featherstitching. Three scalloped flannel petticoats. Three linings in case at that orphanage you wear dark knickers. Three liberty bodices and three nightdresses all fine tucked. And here for Sundays is a petticoat and a pair of drawers edged with lace."

Margaret carefully counted everything. It was all there, as well as the stockings and handkerchiefs, all unworn, just as Hannah had packed them. Margaret hugged the clothes to her.

"Darling, darling Hannah!" she whispered. "I'll find a way to get them. Matron shan't sell them." Then she remembered where she was. It was all very well to say she would find a way to get the clothes, but first how would she find a way to get out of the room?

As she stood there hugging her clothes she heard Mary and Winifred come up the stairs.

"Lucky, lucky them," thought Margaret. "If only I were on the other side of that door!"

She heard the girls go into their room and shut the door. They would probably help her if they could, but how could they break down a door without waking the whole orphanage?

"But I won't give in," Margaret decided. "I'd rather

jump out of the window than have Matron find me here."

Thinking about the window, Margaret moved across to it and looked out. Even the sad-looking garden looked exciting in the moonlight for the shadows were so black. Then Margaret's attention was caught by something. In the garden there was an oak tree, now covered with the beginning of little new leaves. She had always known about the tree but had never thought about it before. It was just a tree with wire netting around it to prevent the orphans from climbing it. But now she saw that it was so tall its top branches were on a level with the third floor. "If only I could get near that tree," Margaret thought, "I would climb down it and then I might find a window open and climb in."

Very quietly, so as not to be heard by Mary and Winifred, she opened the window and leaned out. Then she saw a most extraordinary thing, so extraordinary that it seemed like an answer to a prayer. There was a ladder to the right of the window tied in place by a rope. She could not see where the bottom of the ladder went, but it was clear that some sort of work was being done on the roof.

"And," thought Margaret, "if a workman can climb up then I can climb down."

She took her wicker basket out of the cupboard. "I wonder where she put my skirt and jersey," she thought, "for now I've found a way to get out I shall take everything." Gingerly she turned over the grubby clothes on the table, but her clothes were not among them. So she went back to the cupboards. It was not easy to see what was there, but by fumbling she found there were several garments on hooks, among them her pleated skirt and overcoat. The jersey was at the back of a shelf. Regretfully Margaret hung the coat back on its peg. "I hate leaving it for Matron to sell," she thought, "but I'd never get it into my basket."

It took no time to pack the basket, for the underclothes were already folded. When she had finished Margaret fastened the leather strap. Then, carrying it in one hand while hitching up her detested orphanage nightgown with the other, she sat on the window ledge, swung her legs outside and studied the ladder.

"If I didn't have this basket," she thought, "I could lean over and grab hold of the ladder and pull myself onto it. But with the basket I can't." Then she looked at the oak tree. If she wriggled away from the ladder to the other end of the window sill she would be above the oak tree. Why shouldn't it look after her basket till she could climb up and get it back?

Margaret was so full of schemes that she did not feel frightened. She did not realize how easily she could be killed. So, holding the basket in one hand, she eased herself along the window ledge until she was over the oak tree. Gripping the ledge with her other hand, she threw the basket as hard as she could and, miraculously, it landed safely in the oak tree branches. Fortunately for her, even if a wicker basket hits an oak tree it does not make much noise, so no windows were opened to ask what was going on.

Getting onto the ladder, Margaret found, was more difficult than she had expected. She was, after all, not yet eleven so her legs were not very long. It was more by luck than anything else when, finally despairing of doing it any other way, she propelled herself toward the ladder, caught a rung and somehow held on.

Climbing down the ladder was easy but, wondered Margaret, where was she going? All too soon she found out. The end of the ladder was on a ledge somewhere near the boys' dormitory. She knelt on the ledge and looked down.

"I expect," Margaret thought, "they push another ladder up to here, but they put it away at night." She leaned forward and studied the front of the house. There was nothing to hold onto there.

"I suppose I'll have to stay here until morning," Margaret thought. "Perhaps the workmen start early and will help me down."

It was then for the first time that Margaret looked up. Just above her there was a window and it was open. In a flash she was up the ladder again and had eased the window farther open and climbed in.

The window was at the far end of the corridor outside the boys' dormitory. It would have been easy for Margaret to have slipped down the stairs to the girls' dormitory and then, by rolling along the floor, to have found herself back in her own bed. But that was not good enough for her. She had found the clothes and she meant to hold on to them. So instead of going back to the girls' dormitory she went to the ground floor and let herself out through a side door into the garden.

Getting over the wire netting and climbing the oak tree—especially in her voluminous nightdress—was not easy. But having succeeded so far, Margaret was not going to lose her treasure now, and at the fourth attempt she caught hold of the strap and, pulling the basket with her, reached the ground.

But now what? Where could she hide a basket? If only she knew where Peter kept *David Copperfield*. But all he had said was "out-of-doors somewhere but safe from the rain." Where would you find a place like that in the orphanage? The answer was you wouldn't—at least not big enough for a wicker basket. However, something had to be done with it.

"Just for tonight I'll put it amongst the garden tools," Margaret decided. "I don't believe those are used until the boys get home from school."

The journey back to bed seemed easy after all Margaret had been through. She had a little difficulty in relocking the door into the house for it was stiff, and then she was scared to death because a door opened just as she was climbing the stairs. However, whoever it was did not see her, and almost before she could believe it she was rolling along the dormitory floor to her own bed.

"Margaret Thursday!" her neighbor Chloe whispered. "Where you been? You been gone ever so long."

"No, I haven't," said Margaret, "you've been dreaming." Then, hugging her tin box, she turned over and almost at once she was asleep.

The Archdeacon's Brother

Through Mrs. Tanner the news did reach Lady Corkberry that perhaps all was not as well food-wise as it
should be at the orphanage.

"Mrs. Smedley says she packed enough food for a small
army, m'lady, yet when Lavinia came back it was clear
she had eaten nothing. Ate like a wolf she did, Mrs.
Smedley says."

Lady Corkberry was worried. She herself had nothing
to do with the orphanage, but it was a local charity and,
as such, everybody's concern. She and her friends got
girls from there who were to be trained for domestic
work, and boys for the stables and garden. But she knew
how easy it was to start gossip, so she said quietly:

"Thank you for telling me, Tanner. I will talk to his
lordship and see if inquiries should be made. I daresay

there is nothing in it. At Lavinia's age there is no need to have missed a meal in order to eat like a wolf."

That evening after dinner Lady Corkberry told Lord Corkberry what Mrs. Tanner had told her.

"That the girl was hungry after her walk home would not have worried me, but I had a feeling when Lavinia asked to visit the orphanage every other Sunday that she was anxious about her brothers."

"Is that the girl you spoke to after church?" Lord Corkberry asked.

"That is right."

"I was going to tell you about her. You know I said she was the spittin' image of somebody. Well only this morning it came to me who it was. Do you remember Delaware's daughter Phoebe?"

Lady Phoebe, Lord Delaware's daughter, had caused a great sensation in her day by eloping with one of her father's grooms. Though she had met Phoebe, Lady Corkberry could not remember what she looked like.

"You knew her better than I did for you stayed with them in Ireland for some hunting."

"That's right," Lord Corkberry agreed. "Sixteen she was then, wonderful seat on a horse and pretty as a June rose and wild as a hawk. I told her father, 'You'll have to keep your eye on her,' I said, 'or she'll kick her heels and be off.' And she did, with a groom."

"What happened to them?"

"Nobody knows. Ned Delaware wouldn't have his daughter inside the house—cut her off without a penny. The groom was a bad lot, so I heard."

"Is Lavinia really like her?"

Lord Corkberry nodded.

"Spittin' image. I could see it in spite of that shockin' hat you make the girls wear."

"Curious," said Lady Corkberry. "I wonder if she could be a daughter."

Lord Corkberry shook his head.

"Don't suppose she'd know. Proud as the devil they say Phoebe was. After her father cut her off she never spoke of her family again."

"Then we shall never know. Poor Lavinia, if she is a daughter of Phoebe it's a sad story. But what I was wondering is, just in case there is anything that needs looking into at that orphanage, if we know anybody who is a governor."

Though they had finished dinner they were still at the table, so Lord Corkberry poured himself another glass of port. While he was sipping it he thought over his wife's question.

"I believe old Thomas Windle is."

Thomas Windle was a retired lawyer who lived on land belonging to the Corkberrys.

Lady Corkberry was pleased.

"Good. Then I could call on him and see if he can help."

"I don't really know the fellow except as a tenant," said Lord Corkberry. "But you had better choose your time for they say he never leaves his precious library. Great bookworm the fellow is."

Lady Corkberry sent over a note to Mr. Windle the next morning. She asked if it would be convenient for her to call the following afternoon.

"It is in connection with St. Luke's orphanage that I wish to see you for I understand that you are a governor."

People never refused to see Lady Corkberry so Mr. Windle sent back a note to say he would be delighted to receive her ladyship. But instead of going straight back to the book he was reading he thought about the orphanage. There were governors' meetings four times a year which he attended faithfully, so it wasn't that which was worrying him but something else. Now what? Then it came to him. His brother, the archdeacon. He had asked him to sponsor an orphan. Now what was its name, was it a girl or a boy? He went to his desk and searched for his brother's letters. There they were. Margaret Thursday, of course! He had written several times about the child's admittance. She must be in the orphanage by now. Could Lady Corkberry have come across her and felt he had been remiss? He did hope not for he believed he took his duties as a governor seriously. Oh well, he would know tomorrow and if he had been remiss he would atone for it in any way Lady Corkberry might suggest.

When Lady Corkberry drove over the next afternoon Mr. Windle met her on the doorstep. After greeting her he said:

"My library is the most pleasant room in the house. Should we talk in there?"

It was a delicious day with birds singing and the smell of flowers blowing on a light breeze.

"Why should we go indoors?" she asked. "I see you have a seat under these delightful lilac trees. Why do we not sit there?"

Under the lilac trees Lady Corkberry explained why she was worried. Then she said:

"The orphanage as such is none of my business, but orphaned children are the business of us all. Are you satisfied with the way the place is run?"

Mr. Windle was a thin man, pale from spending too much time in his library. Now he nervously rubbed his hands together, which made the joints crack.

"I must explain that we governors meet only four times a year. These meetings are largely concerned with finance. It costs a great deal of money to feed and house a hundred orphans."

"I am sure," Lady Corkberry agreed. "I will tell Lord Corkberry we must increase our subscription."

"Too kind," murmured Mr. Windle. "Of course we see the matron, who they say is an admirable woman." He sighed. "I'm ashamed to say she frightens me."

"And you only see her—nobody else?"

"No. Matron reports on conditions generally and the boys and girls who have gone out to work. You see, Lady Corkberry, there is a ladies' committee. It meets monthly and it is they who inspect the home and hear about the individual children. I thought perhaps you had come about that for I sponsored a child called Margaret Thursday. She was highly recommended by my brother. He is an archdeacon."

Mrs. Tanner had not added the postscript about Margaret Thursday without asking Lady Corkberry's permission.

"How curious! Margaret Thursday is a friend of my new scullery maid, Lavinia Beresford, who has two brothers in the orphanage. I am sure there is no excuse for the uneasiness I feel, but all the same would it not be pleasant to know we had nothing to be uneasy about? Do you think we could hatch a little plot together? As this child is your responsibility, could you perhaps invite her here to your house? Children talk so much more freely away from an institutional background."

Mr. Windle was appalled.

"A child here! I'm afraid I'm an old bachelor, Lady Corkberry, and have no idea how to entertain a child."

Lady Corkberry almost patted his hand.

"I would not suggest she come here alone. I should like Lavinia—she is my scullery maid—and her brothers to be invited too. I believe the younger boy is very small and small children confide in one in a way older children would not. Now if you could invite Margaret Thursday and the Beresford boys on a Sunday afternoon I could arrange that the elder sister, Lavinia, could have time off to meet them. Lord Corkberry and I might look in during the afternoon."

What could poor Mr. Windle do? Lady Corkberry was not a person to whom you said "No." So half an hour later when she drove away he was holding a piece of paper on which was written:

"Margaret Thursday and the Beresford boys. Tea one Sunday. Purpose—inquiring into feeding in the orphanage. Lady C. says she will provide cakes."

The Invitation

Margaret found it very hard to get up on the morning after her adventure. She had not noticed at the time how much like a monkey she had been forced to act, so she was surprised at how many parts of her ached. Chloe, who was sure she had not been dreaming and that Margaret really had left the dormitory during the night, looked at her suspiciously.

"What's the matter? Why don't you get up? Old Jones won't half create if she sees you."

Stifling groans, Margaret got as far as sitting on the edge of the bed.

"I don't feel too good."

"Shall I tell old Jones you're sick?"

That suggestion got Margaret out of bed and, with toothbrush and mug in hand, into the washroom queue.

"I was only pretending," she told Chloe. To herself she said: "If I was half dead I'd get to the school somehow. I don't want to be here when Matron finds that basket is missing."

As it turned out, the basket had to stay hidden under the gardener's tools for it was a relentlessly wet morning and there was no possible excuse for anyone to go near the garden. But the moment she reached school Margaret told Peter about it.

"Well, after I got my basket I couldn't think where to put it so I put it under the garden tools. Nobody will touch those before you boys do, will they?"

Peter, who had been listening to Margaret's story with the spellbound interest he gave to reading, woke up at that.

"Oh yes. Mr. Toms does." Then he looked at the window. "But not today he wouldn't, not in this rain. He keeps special jobs, he says, for wet days."

"Could you get it, do you think?"

"I expect so," Peter agreed, "but where would I put it?"

The children looked at each other. Where could Margaret hide it? Even if she unpacked the basket there was no place safe from Matron's and Miss Jones's prying eyes.

"In those sheds where you boys cut wood is there hay or anything like that?"

Polly was ringing the bell, so there could be no more talk until recess. To Margaret's surprise, Peter gave her arm a nice kind squeeze as if to say "don't worry." He said:

"Leave it to me. I'll tell you later."

At recess time Peter pulled Margaret into a corner of the schoolroom for it was too wet to go outside. It was easy for the orphans to talk to one another undisturbed during recess for the village children usually sat together eating what they called "beavers," which was a midmorning snack.

"I think I know where I can put it," Peter whispered. "It's not hay exactly, more sort of dried sticks which I think Mr. Toms uses when he grows peas. It's under them I keep *David Copperfield*. I think Mr. Toms knows and doesn't mind."

"Could you put it there at dinnertime? For I expect that by the time we get home this afternoon Matron will find it's gone and there won't half be a search."

Peter considered that.

"If it goes on raining it's all right where it is until tomorrow. Directly it's fine I can move it because it's one of my tasks to clean and polish the spades, so I can say I was doing that."

Margaret hated to leave the basket where somebody might find it by accident, but Peter seemed to know what he was talking about. In fact, that morning Peter stopped being a little boy and felt older than she did. So, unusually meekly for her, Margaret said:

"All right. I'll leave it to you."

To Margaret's surprise there was no excitement when they got back to the orphanage that afternoon. Why wasn't there, she wondered? Hadn't Sally's mother told Matron there was no basket in the cupboard? Then she found a reason. Most likely Matron had only told Sally's mother to mend and wash the clothes on the table. It could be she never even looked in the cupboards. Anyway, whatever had happened it was clear there was no search going on. But though there was no search there was obviously something else in the air for Matron, during tea, gave Margaret what she described later to Chloe as bite-you-in-the-back looks.

After tea, as usual, Matron gave out chores. Some of the boys, Margaret noticed, were given repair jobs to do in the house, but others were to put on their cloaks and run to the outhouse where Mr. Toms had work for them to do.

"We have had," Matron said, "as possibly some of you have noticed, workmen repairing the roof. This is now finished and Mr. Toms will order some of you to clean the ladder the men used."

"My goodness!" thought Margaret. "Wasn't I lucky! If it was tonight I was getting my basket the ladder wouldn't have been there and it would have been raining."

The girls' tasks were much as usual, though that evening there was a sewing class. This meant that those, like Margaret, who had to peel potatoes had less time in which to do it.

"But," said Matron, "though you may have less time, I shall expect every potato to be peeled, so no talking. Any girl found talking will have to deal with me. Dismiss—but will you, Margaret Thursday, stay here. I want to speak to you."

In pity, Margaret's friends—and she had many by now —looked at her. What had she done? What would her punishment be? For themselves the potato peelers felt punished already, for potato peeling, which had become popular since Margaret had come to the orphanage, would be very dull without her stories to keep them going.

Margaret felt as if cold water was trickling down her

spine. So Matron had found out! Now what would she do to her?

Matron, more red-faced than usual, beckoned Margaret to stand in front of her.

"I suppose you have no idea what I am going to say to you?"

Margaret tried not to show how frightened she was. She stuck her chin in the air.

"No."

"You came to us, if you remember, through the recommendation of one of our governors—Mr. Windle."

Margaret turned a mental somersault. Mr. Windle! So this wasn't about the missing basket!

"Well really," she explained, "it wasn't because of Mr. Windle but because of my rector. He was the one who found me with three of everything of the very best quality on the church steps—his archdeacon wrote to his brother and it's he who is Mr. Windle."

Matron's rather beady black eyes gave a sort of snap.

"You talk too much. Kindly listen in silence when I am speaking. Mr. Windle feels it is time he saw you since he sponsored you. Today a servant rode over with a note. He wishes you and the two Beresford boys—at I understand the request of Lady Corkberry—to take tea with him on Sunday. A conveyance will be sent for you at 2:30."

Margaret gaped at Matron. Going out to tea! A conveyance might mean a carriage! How glorious to go out to tea in a carriage. She would feel like a princess. Then she remembered what Matron was waiting for. She gave a little curtsy.

"Thank you, Matron."

"Do not thank me," said Matron. "You are one of my most unsatisfactory children and if I had my way you would have no treats at all. I disapprove utterly of you being allowed out two Sundays running. But since Mr. Windle is a governor I must respect his wishes. One thing I must demand of you—under no circumstances discuss orphanage affairs. Just say 'I am very happy.' If you say more be sure I shall hear of it."

Margaret thought, "Catch me telling a lie like that. I'm certain Peter and Horatio won't either." But, looking as meek as she knew how, she gave another bob.

"Yes, Matron. I quite understand, Matron."

In the scullery she confided in whispers to her fellow-peelers what Matron had said. When she came to "just say I am very happy," the children giggled so much that a terrified Mary, who was in charge, rushed in.

"Oh, do be quiet or someone will hear, and if they do Matron will take it out on me. You know she will."

That evening after sewing, Margaret, as she often did, sneaked into the playroom to see how Horatio was getting on. He was managing much better now that Ben was given sweets by Peter not to put soap in his eyes. He seldom came down to breakfast red-eyed and shiny with tears. He was, too, getting on well with the other children, for being small for his age he was in great demand to be the baby when the little girls played "Home." That evening when Margaret came in he was being the baby rocked to sleep in a chair. But he stopped being the baby when he saw Margaret and ran to her. He pulled at her arm to make her lean down so he could whisper.

"Peter said if I saw you I was to say . . ." Horatio took a deep breath and recited like a budgerigar: "He got out and he has hidden it."

Margaret kissed him.

"Thank you, darling. Do you know we are going out to tea again this Sunday? I must go now or Matron will catch me."

The little girls came to put Horatio back in his "bed." He beamed at them.

"Do you know last Sunday when Vinia came we had so much to eat we couldn't eat any more and now Margaret says it's going to happen again. Next Sunday."

The peeky, pinched-looking little girls were pleased for him.

"Lucky you!" one of them said. "I never had so much to eat I couldn't eat no more. It must be a lovely feeling."

Horatio patted his tummy.

"Oh, it is. It's the bestest feeling in the whole world."

Questions

Lavinia was delighted when Mrs. Tanner told her the news about Mr. Windle's tea party.

"There's a trap being sent for the children at half past two," Mrs. Tanner explained. "So her ladyship said to tell you that if you left the house about three you should be there in nice time. You're a very lucky girl, Lavinia. It isn't many in your position would be allowed out two Sundays running."

"Oh, I do know that, Mrs. Tanner, ma'am," Lavinia agreed. "I do indeed. Would you thank her ladyship for me?"

Mrs. Tanner was herself puzzled by what she had to say next. She never criticized anything Lady Corkberry did, but this time she felt her charity was going too far. That this was how she felt showed in her voice.

"You will have the opportunity to do that yourself. Her ladyship has stated she wishes to see you in her sitting room at 2:30 this afternoon. One of the men will show you the way."

Lavinia was as puzzled as Mrs. Tanner. Why should Lady Corkberry wish to see her? The new scullery maid! It didn't make sense. She spoke her thoughts out loud.

"Perhaps I am to be told who this Mr. Windle may be and why he has invited myself and the boys for the afternoon, for truly, Mrs. Tanner, ma'am, I have never heard of him."

"No doubt," Mrs. Tanner agreed, though what she thought was, if telling things to a maid needs to be done it should be done through me. Out loud she said: "Now back to your work and do not forget the sitting room at 2:30 sharp in a clean apron and, of course, a cap."

Caps were the bane of Lavinia's life. They were seldom worn in the kitchen, but they had to be at hand for morning prayers and in case Lady Corkberry came in person to speak to Mrs. Smedley. They were not the starched caps worn by the parlor and housemaids, but little round pieces of linen edged with lace. Lavinia did try always to put her cap where she could find it, but more often than not it got mislaid and all too often trodden underfoot. As a result, often before prayers she had to wash it out and dry it on a toasting fork in front of the stove.

That morning she took Clara into her confidence.

"I must give my cap a wash," she said as she searched the back of the scullery door. "I'm sure I hung it here after prayers."

Clara came to help.

"What you want it for now?"

Lavinia pounced on her cap which had fallen on the floor and got caught under the door.

"Oh, look at it! Like a dish rag!" She ran to the sink and began washing it. "I have to go to the sitting room to see Lady Corkberry at half-past two."

Clara nearly dropped the mincer she was cleaning.

"Whatever for? What you done? Never once have I been sent to speak to her ladyship, and if I had been sent for me mum wouldn't half wallop me."

Lavinia went on washing her cap.

"I don't think I've done anything, it's about Sunday. A man called Mr. Windle has invited my brothers for Sunday afternoon and I'm to go too, and Mrs. Tanner said when I saw her ladyship to be sure to wear a clean apron and a cap."

Clara was surprised.

"Mr. Windle! He lives in what they call the Dower House. My dad says he's got ever such a lot of money but he spends it all on books. He doesn't care about nothin' else. Catch me buying books if I had a lot of money!"

Lavinia had washed the cap.

"I'll just slip out and peg it up outside. It should be dry long before dinnertime."

At 2:30 sharp one of the footmen opened Lady Corkberry's sitting-room door.

"It is the young person from the scullery, m'lady."

Lady Corkberry was writing letters. She got up from her desk and sat in an armchair.

"Come in, Lavinia." She nodded to the footman. "You may go, Henry."

Lavinia, in a clean print dress, an apron so starched it crackled, and her cap pinned to the top of her head, stood respectfully just inside the door after her curtsy. She thought she had never seen a more beautiful room. There were huge windows with rose-sprigged curtains and a rose-colored carpet. The furniture shone so that it reflected the sunlight. On all suitable furniture there were bowls of flowers, and many of the chairs and the sofa were covered in the same material as the curtains.

Lady Corkberry cleared her throat. Lavinia had been on her conscience ever since Lord Corkberry had told her whose daughter she might be. She wanted to find out what Lavinia knew about her background, but she did not know where to start.

"You have been told about the tea party at Mr. Windle's to which your brothers have been invited?"

Lavinia gave another curtsy.

"Yes, m'lady. It is so good of him for I do not think he has ever heard of my brothers."

Lady Corkberry thought, "She really could be Lord Delaware's granddaughter." Aloud she said:

"No, indeed. It is your little friend Margaret Thursday whom he knows. His brother is, I understand, an archdeacon. It was he who suggested sending Margaret Thursday to the orphanage."

"That was a mean thing to do," thought Lavinia. Out loud she said:

"I see, m'lady."

Lady Corkberry thought she saw an opening.

"You sound doubtful that it was a kindness. Do you not care for the orphanage?"

Lavinia was not going to risk any trouble coming to the boys while they were under Matron's care, and there would be trouble if Matron thought she had been making complaints.

"I daresay it's very good, m'lady," she said, "but of course it's not like being in your own home."

Lady Corkberry nodded.

"No, indeed. Have you children been orphaned long?"
Lavinia thought before she answered and chose her
words with care.

"Our mother died at Christmas. From that time until
the boys went to the orphanage I managed our home."

"But it was too much for a young girl?" Lady Corkberry suggested.

Lavinia pictured their home in her mind's eye. It had
been small but her mother had kept it wonderfully and
somehow, in spite of the poor furniture, had managed a
sort of elegance and, still more remarkable since they
lived in London, had seen to it there were nearly always
some fresh flowers in vases. Lavinia had done her best to
keep the house as spotless as her mother had done and to
continue the boys' lessons, but the money had given out.
Her mother had managed to keep the home going by selling such nice things as she had, but when she died there
were no nice things left and almost no money.

"Your mother starved herself to keep you children
going," the doctor had told Lavinia, "which was why she
had no strength to fight an illness. You can't manage on
your own, you know."

Desperate at the thought of breaking up the family,
Lavinia had pleaded with the doctor.

"I can manage. I can get work, I'm very strong."

Unwillingly the doctor had given in, but only temporarily .

"I won't interfere now, I'll give you a month. If at the
end of that time you aren't fixed up I must see that some
arrangement is made for you."

At the end of the month when the doctor called things
were no better—in fact, worse. Lavinia had not found

regular work and Horatio was crying because he was hungry.

"I've had a talk with the vicar of this parish whom you know," the doctor told Lavinia. "He knows of an orphanage that will take the boys and find you a place in service nearby. Meanwhile, I will lend you the money to live on. After you have left I can sell what is in the house to pay me back so do not worry about that."

The vicar made all the arrangements. He had not known Mrs. Beresford except by sight when she brought the children to church on Sundays, but he could say with truth that the boys appeared entirely suitable for a church orphanage.

"There is just one point," the vicar had told Lavinia. "To go to St. Luke's the boys must be orphans. When did your father die? I don't remember seeing him."

Lavinia had turned a little white, but she spoke out bravely.

"No, you would not have. He never came to church. He died nearly a year before my mother did."

Lavinia's thoughts came back to Lady Corkberry. What was it she had asked? Oh yes, she had asked if they had given up their home because it had been too much for her to run.

"No, m'lady. But it was not a neighborhood where there was much work so the money was finished."

"Had your mother worked?"

Lavinia thought again of her mother and the thinking brought tears to her eyes. She looked at the floor, hoping Lady Corkberry would not notice.

"No, m'lady, but she taught us all our lessons. That's how it is my brother Peter is such a reader. Somehow she always managed to get him books."

Lady Corkberry felt she was asking too many questions and she could see that questions about her mother upset Lavinia, but she had to persist.

"Was your mother widowed long?"

Lavinia again gazed at the floor, but this time it was for fear her expression would give something away.

"No, not long."

Lady Corkberry sighed. She had found out nothing and perhaps had upset the girl. She gave Lavinia a dismissing nod.

"Well, I must not keep you from your duties. It is possible that his lordship and I may be at Mr. Windle's on Sunday, in which case I may see you then."

"What did her ladyship want?" Clara asked the moment Lavinia got back to the kitchen.

Lavinia took off her cap and clean apron.

"I don't know really, except to say how it was that my brothers are asked to Mr. Windle's place. It's on account of another orphan called Margaret Thursday. I suppose he thought it would be easier seeing her if she had other children to play with."

"She was a long time telling you that," said Clara.

Lavinia thought over her interview.

"Well, she asked a lot of questions, you know—about where we lived before the orphanage and all that."

Clara nodded.

"The gentry are all like that. If they was us they'd be called nosy. Come on, old mother Smedley said we could go out in the grounds for an hour."

Jem was sent to fetch the children for the coachmen liked
to have their Sundays off. The coachmen at Sedgecombe
Place were always very well turned out in fawn coats,
white breeches and black top hats with what looked like
a little windmill on the side. Jem had no uniform as such
for he never drove the Corkberrys, but the head coachman had strong views on how his stable lads should appear when in public. So it was a spruced-up Jem who
drew up the trap smartly outside the orphanage. He was
dressed in a navy coat which had belonged to the head
groom and had been cut down for him, and a blue

peaked cap rather like that worn by chauffeurs today.

The children, hopping from one foot to the other with excitement, were waiting for him, but as the trap stopped, Miss Jones flew out of the front door like a Jack-in-the-box.

"Quietly, children," she said in her most repressive voice. "Horatio, you will sit in front with the driver and you two will sit in the back. And no talking or you will take this young man's attention from his work."

Like anybody else given charge of a vehicle, Jem looked upon it as his property while he drove it. Until Miss Jones spoke he had not cared twopence who sat where, but she had rubbed him the wrong way and he decided not to put up with the old cat's interference. Speaking as though he had been given orders by Lady Corkberry herself, he said,

"It's the little girl who is to come in front. The boys are to sit at the back."

Miss Jones was furious but she said nothing. "It is extraordinary," she thought, "how things are always working out well for Margaret Thursday. But let her wait—one day we shall knock the spirit out of her."

As they drove off, Margaret looked at Jem out of the corners of her eyes and decided that she liked him, but she wanted to be sure he didn't despise her for living in an orphanage. She spread her brown skirt out as elegantly as she could.

"You mustn't think I'm an ordinary orphan," she explained. "You see, I was found on a Thursday on the steps of the church with three of everything of the very best quality."

Jem grinned.

"I wasn't. I was born on a canal boat and I'd be there still if I hadn't had pneumonia."

Margaret was thrilled.

"In a boat! Do you know it's the first time I ever met anybody born on a boat. Doesn't it make you feel special?"

Jem grinned again.

"No, why should it? Six of us there is, but we've all left the boat now except for my young brother Tom and he'd like to but he can't get away."

"Why can't he?"

"A canal boat is pulled by a 'orse, see? Well, with me dad steering, someone 'as to lead the 'orse and Tom's all that's left."

"Doesn't he like leading the horse?"

Jem shook his head.

"Would you like to be a legger—that's what we call 'em? Hour after hour leadin' the 'orse in all weathers? Cruel it could be when there was wind and rain. But when it snowed!"

"I wouldn't mind," said Margaret. "I wouldn't mind anything as much as living in that old orphanage. Some-day I'll run away."

Jem looked at her clothes.

"You wouldn't get far dolled up like that."

For a second Margaret nearly told him about her bas-ket, but caution won.

"I've got plans," she said.

Jem had decided Margaret was a proper card so he teased her.

"Well, when you run away give me a knock and I'll start you on your road."

Quite seriously Margaret answered:

"I will. What is your name and where do you live?"

Still amused by her, Jem told her.

"I'm Jem. There's bedrooms over the stables. I'm the last so you can't miss it. I've 'ung a 'orseshoe over the door."

Though he was used to appearing in the law courts, Mr. Windle was not used to entertaining children, but he came out the moment his manservant reported that the trap had arrived. He had the sort of face people connect with the law—a mixture of cleverness and shrewdness overlaid by a mask, so that whoever he was cross-examining would not know what to expect. Now he tried to drop his mask and appear pleased, but it was not a great success for he still looked like what the rector used to describe to Margaret when speaking of his churchwarden as "a cold fish."

He gave Margaret his hands to help her down.

"Welcome, my child!"

Then he turned to lift down Horatio.

"And how are you, my little man?"

"Not very well at this moment," said Horatio. "I think if the drive had gone on any longer I should have been as sick as sick."

"I think it's riding with his back to the horses, sir," Peter explained. "You know, seeing the road running away from you."

The manservant was helping Peter down. He did not care for charity children and looked as though he didn't.

"Don't you trouble, sir. I'll take them round to the back to tidy themselves."

Mr. Windle looked relieved for certainly the boys did

appear pale and it really would be distressing if they were sick in the driveway.

"Very good, Gregson, and tell Mrs. Gregson to look after Margaret. Afterwards send them out in the garden to play. I will go back to the library."

Peter looked after him longingly.

"Has he a library?" he asked Gregson. "I mean a real one full of books?"

Gregson looked down his nose.

"We have some thousands of books here. We have the finest library in the county."

Jem winked at the children, then he tossed them their capes.

"I don't suppose you'll need those, but you may as well have them just in case."

Washed and brushed, the children had only just reached the garden via the back door when Lavinia arrived. She looked pretty for she had let down her hair and wore it tied back with a ribbon. Also, she had taken off her Sunday black and was wearing a green dress her mother had made for her. It was a little tight and short, but it still suited her.

"Darlings!" she called. "Come here and let me look at you all."

Horatio flung himself at her.

"Vinia! Vinia! I was nearly sick driving here but I'm all better now."

Lavinia was carrying a basket. She drew back a cloth which covered its contents.

"Just as well you're all better for look at what there is for tea."

The children gasped for the basket contained the most

wonderful assortment of cakes.

"Could we have just one now?" Horatio begged.

But Lavinia pulled the cloth back into place.

"No. You'd get me the sack. Mrs. Smedley—she's the head cook—packed the basket herself and said I was to take it straight to Mrs. Gregson. Do you know where I find her?"

"I'll show you," Margaret offered. "We go in at the back door. She says the front door is not for the likes of us."

Lavinia laughed.

"What do we care! Are you boys coming too?"

To Lavinia's surprise it was Peter who said "No."

"I thought Horry and I would explore."

Lavinia looked around. There were neat flower-beds full of tulips, wallflowers and forget-me-nots, all of which looked as if the distance between them had been measured by a tape measure. The wide lawns were neatly mowed and the paths spotlessly kept. This was no run-about garden at all.

"There's not much to explore," Lavinia said doubtfully. "I think it's the sort of place where you sit out of the wind and talk. Imagine how awful it would be if you fell over a rose bush and broke it."

Horatio had sharp eyes, and now he pointed to where the garden ended.

"I can see a place to explore. There's a little gate in that wall."

Lavinia accepted that.

"All right—off you go. Come on, Margaret."

To Horatio's disappointment, Peter refused to go to the gate in the wall.

"We'll go there presently, but now I want to walk around the house."

"What for?"

Peter was vague.

"Just to look. I want to know where the rooms are."

Mrs. Gregson unbent a little toward Lavinia for she loved news of what went on at Sedgecombe Place. With admiration she unpacked the cakes.

"Wonderful hand with cakes Mrs. Smedley has. I could, of course, have made them here, but there's enough work for me without fancy stuff. I suppose she gets her fancy stuff started early—I mean meringues and all that?"

Lavinia wanted to get out to join the boys, but she did not intend to make an enemy for, after all, Mr. Windle was a governor at the orphanage, so she stayed chatting for a few minutes.

Outside, Margaret said to her:

"Don't call the boys for a minute. I must, I absolutely must tell you about what's happened. I've got my basket back and all my clothes."

Margaret was so enthralled with the story she was telling that neither she nor Lavinia saw Lord and Lady Corkberry come in through a gate which led into their park, nor did they hear them as they crossed the lawn. So both jumped when Lady Corkberry said:

"There you are, Lavinia, and this must be Margaret Thursday."

Both girls gave a curtsy.

"Yes, m'lady," Lavinia said hurriedly, feeling sure that Margaret would not know who Lady Corkberry was or how to address her.

"Where are your brothers?" Lady Corkberry asked.

Lavinia looked around.

"I don't know, m'lady, but they can't be far, for it isn't a very big garden." Then she raised her voice and called: "Peter! Horry!"

Just out of sight Horatio tugged at Peter's arm.

"Come on, Peter, Vinia's calling us, and anyway it's very rude to stand on tiptoe so you can see into someone's window. Mummy told me that."

"You go," Peter whispered. "I must see a little more. I won't be a minute, I promise you. But don't tell Lavinia what I'm doing."

Obediently, Horatio trotted around the corner.

"There you are," said Lavinia. "Where's Peter?"

"Coming." Horatio gazed at Lord Corkberry. "Who are you?"

Lord Corkberry put his hand under Horatio's chin and stared down at him.

"I'm Lord Corkberry, but the question is—who are you?"

"I am Horatio Beresford," Horry explained.

Lord Corkberry turned to Lady Corkberry.

"He's Ned to the life. Never saw anythin' like it."

As Lady Corkberry had hoped, Horatio proved easy to get information out of. She soon learned that he wanted to see what was on the other side of the gate in the wall so she offered to show him. Hand in hand they walked across the lawn, while Lord Corkberry went to greet Mr. Windle.

"Do you like living in the orphanage, Horatio?" Lady Corkberry asked.

Horatio looked surprised.

"Of course not. Nobody does."

"Why? Are they unkind?"

Horatio thought about that.

"Ben was. He always put soap in my eyes on purpose until Vinia sent him sweets not to."

"Do you get plenty to eat?"

Horatio was amazed at such ignorance.

"In the orphanage there is hardly nothing to eat. There's very nasty porridge, all lumps, for breakfast, and teeny-weeny milk and never any sugar. Then for dinner

there's meant to be meat but mostly it's carrots and
things. For supper there's just two pieces of stale bread
and cocoa."

Lady Corkberry hoped that perhaps Horatio was ex-
aggerating. It was natural for children to complain about
food.

"You don't look starved."

"That is because of school," Horatio explained. "I eat
there. Polly Jenkin brings me things."

"And who is Polly Jenkin?"

Horatio was surprised.

"I thought everybody knew her. She helps Miss
Snelston."

Lady Corkberry saw daylight.

"And Miss Snelston is your schoolteacher?"

"Of course she is."

They had reached the gate so Horatio peered through.
Outside was the canal bank and by squinting sideways
Horatio could see quite a lot of the canal. Lady Cork-
berry shook the gate.

"I'm afraid Mr. Windle keeps this locked, and very
wise too, for you never know who's about near canals. Do
you like the matron at the orphanage?"

Horatio swung round. His eyes, Lady Corkberry noticed, had dilated with fear.

"No," he whispered, as if even in this garden Matron
could hear. "She frightens everybody. She beats Margaret
and locks her in a dark cupboard full of black beetles. It's
because of Matron that everyone is so miserable."

From Margaret's, Peter's and Horatio's point of view
the tea was magnificent, but they ate so much and took so
long over it that as soon as it was finished Lord and Lady

Corkberry and Lavinia had to leave. This meant that
Mr. Windle, much to his dismay, was in charge of the
children for a quarter of an hour until Jem brought the
trap around. Fortunately for Mr. Windle, Horatio asked
if he had a key to the gate in the canal bank. He did have
so he, Horatio and Margaret had a look at the canal and
were rewarded by seeing a dabchick and all her babies
swim by.

"Where's your brother?" Mr. Windle asked Horatio.

What Horatio might have answered Mr. Windle was
never to know for Margaret, always the first to reply,
said:

"Oh, he will be mooning about somewhere. He's a terrible dreamer but he's never lost."

Walking home, Lady Corkberry said to Lord Corkberry:

"I've talked to the little boy. There is something
wrong at that orphanage. Next week I shall call upon the
schoolmistress and see what she knows or suspects. From
what little Horatio said I have a feeling that the matron
is a bad woman, in which case she must be punished."

Lord Corkberry nodded:

"And I have a feelin' I shall have to go to Ireland and
have it out with Ned Delaware. If young Horatio isn't his
grandson I'll eat my hat."

To avoid further trouble with his insides, Horatio was put in the front seat between Margaret and Jem. Margaret offered to give her seat to Peter, but he wouldn't have it. He was in his most dreamy mood and scarcely seemed to be conscious of his surroundings. He settled down in the back seat muffled in his brown cloak, and only after a nudge from Margaret and much fumbling did he produce his hand for Mr. Windle to shake.

Horatio slept all the way home, and even Margaret, because she was full of good food and air, was almost silent. It was not until they could see the orphanage that she became her animated self.

"Doesn't it look awful, Jem? But it's much awfuller inside. I shouldn't wonder if Matron was waiting to pounce on me for something I haven't done the second I get in. Thank goodness I'm still full of tea, so I shan't mind if I have to go to bed without supper."

Horatio had awoken and clung pathetically to Margaret.

"Must we go in that horrid place? I wish we could have stayed with Vinia."

Margaret hugged him and tried to think of something to say to comfort him. She turned around to Peter.

"Do you suppose directly we get in Matron will find us Sunday tasks or do you think I could look after Horatio?"

"Matron's not going to get a chance with me," Peter answered. "I'm going straight to the shed to see if the others are working. If Matron asks, that is where I am. But I am sure you will get a task."

At the orphanage door Margaret said good-by to Jem.

"Thank you very much for driving us and telling me about living on a canal boat." She lowered her voice. "And if ever I do run away I'll come to you first. The last bedroom over the stables."

Though he was certain Margaret did not mean it, Jem winked in a conspiratorial way.

"And don't forget—feel for me 'orseshoe over the door."

The moment she and Horatio were inside the orphanage Margaret could smell trouble. By the rules laid down by the ladies' committee there should not have been tasks on Sundays, but there usually were for Matron was a firm believer in Satan finding mischief for idle hands. Having hung her own and Horatio's cloak in the cloakroom, Margaret was wondering if she dared slip into the little ones' playroom when Violet, looking as scared as a rabbit, sidled into the room.

Margaret despised Violet, considering her a poor spiritless thing. But she had given her one of the sweets meant for Ben to make up for her having been whipped when she had mistaken Margaret for a burglar, so she approached her as a friend.

"What's up? Where is everybody?"

Violet reduced her voice to a scared squeak.

"I don't know where everybody is but Matron's proper upset. I think you're meant to be in the scullery."

Margaret took Horatio into the hall and gave him a push toward the playroom.

"In there, darling. Go and play 'Homes' until supper."

In the scullery she found the usual potato peelers, including Susan and Chloe. They were not peeling potatoes but sitting around a tub scrubbing turnips. They were all pleased to see Margaret.

"Did you 'ave a good time?" Susan whispered.

In an almost inaudible voice another girl said:

"Tell us about the eats."

Margaret saw that the other girls had taken off their Sunday fichus and had rolled up their sleeves so she did the same.

"There is no need to whisper," she said cheerfully. "There's no one in the kitchen, not even Winifred."

The girls were sitting on benches, and they made room for Margaret on one.

"You better go careful," they told her. "Matron's in a terrible taking."

Margaret kicked the basket of turnips.

"Where did this lot come from?"

"One of the farmers sent them in," Chloe explained. "I think he grew them for lambing but he had this lot over."

Margaret inspected the turnips.

"I guess the sheep wouldn't eat them and I don't blame them—half of them are rotten."

"What won't fatten will fill," said Susan.

This was such a favorite statement of Matron's that the girls giggled.

"What's Matron in a taking about?" Margaret asked.

"We don't rightly know," Chloe said. "We think from the way she carried on something's been stolen from up there." She jerked her thumb toward the roof.

"You know," one of the other girls whispered. "It's that room up top opposite where Mary and Winifred sleep. It's where Matron keeps you-know-what."

Margaret was able to get away with a nod in reply. Her heart was beating so hard she could scarcely speak. At last she managed: "Who is she creating about? Did she say?"

"No," the girls told her. "She just created about everything. It was Winifred told us something was missing. She heard her banging around in the room upstairs mutterin' something awful."

Chloe nudged Margaret.

"And we said lucky Margaret's out or Matron would take it out on her same as she always does."

Susan said:

"Come on, Margaret, tell us what it was like and what you 'ad to eat."

Margaret somehow pulled herself together. The girls had looked forward to her getting back and she was not going to let them down.

"Well, first the carriage came for us with a man dressed all proper driving. Old Jones didn't half look mad to see me sitting up beside him."

"Tell us about what you ate," Chloe pleaded.

"You wait," said Margaret. "Well, we came to the house and there was Mr. Windle and a manservant waiting. And do you know what? The maid curtsied to me and said 'Good afternoon, Miss Thursday.' "

The girls giggled, well aware Margaret was making things up, but enjoying it just the same.

"Then," Margaret went on, "after we'd washed we were sent to play in the garden. You never saw a garden like it. Why, it was so big you could lose yourself. And the flowers! Roses and lilies and everything."

Winifred poked her head around the door.

"Funny sort of garden in April, but do talk quiet. Matron's creatin' somethin' shockin' and she'll kill me if she hears you talking."

Margaret lowered her voice to the smallest whisper.

"The tea! Well, there were rolls with real cream and jam on them and then cakes. Well, you never saw anything like it, all iced and with cherries on, and covered in chocolate. And inside was whipped cream."

It was too much for the girls. Together they let out an envious "Ooh!"

Matron must have been passing for in one second she was in the scullery. Her face was redder than usual and her hair seemed to be standing on end.

"Who dared to make that noise?" She looked around at the girls and saw Margaret. "I did not tell you to come in here. You should have reported to Miss Jones as soon as you came in and she would have told you that I wished to see you. Come with me."

Matron strode out of the room, and with apparent meekness Margaret followed, though making time to give the girls a wink to cover the fact that her knees were shaking.

Matron led Margaret into her office and, shutting the door, sat down behind her desk.

"Lift up your skirt, Margaret," she ordered.

Scared as she was, Margaret found it hard not to smile. So that was what Matron wanted. Was she really hoping to see a petticoat edged with lace? She lifted her skirt to display her gray orphanage petticoat.

"It was clean this morning."

The orphans always had clean underclothes on Sundays so Matron ignored that.

"Now lift up that petticoat."

Margaret's chin shot into the air. This was really going too far. Drawers weren't clothes you showed people. However, it was not worth being beaten for, so slowly she lifted her petticoat to show her coarse long drawers.

Even Matron could see that there was nothing hidden under them. Politely, Margaret held out one leg.

"Would you like me to take off my boots?"

Though she had tried to tell herself that Margaret had stolen the wicker basket, Matron did not really believe that she had. How would she have known where it was and, having found it, where could she have hidden it? No, without doubt the culprit must be that woman she had employed to wash and mend the old clothes she was taking north to sell. But it was not going to be easy to prove. How could the woman have carried a basket out of the orphanage without being spotted? And if she was accused without evidence to whom might she not complain? And suppose she, the Matron, complained to the ladies' committee—how was she to explain why she was having the clothes repaired at her own expense? As usual she turned her bad temper on to Margaret.

"You can put down your skirt. It was you, of course,

who led the girls on to make that noise in the scullery—it
is always you. We have had nothing but trouble since you
came to the orphanage."

Margaret, furious at having been made to stand in
front of Matron in a pair of shameful orphanage drawers,
felt as if that mother whom she had never known was en-
couraging her to assert herself. Chin high and cheeks
flushed, she retorted:

"I do not mean to cause trouble, I think it's just that I
am used to better things. You may not know, but when
my mother left me on the church steps I had three of everything of the very best quality embroidered with
crowns"—this was a new invention and pleased her—
"and each year gold money was left to keep me."

Matron asked in an icy voice:

"And what happens to the money now?"

"It stopped. You see my mother got quite poor, for my
father, who was an admiral, was drowned on the high
seas."

Matron had had enough. She seized Margaret by the
arm and led her back to the scullery. There she snatched
a greasy, dirty dishrag from the sink and shoved it into
Margaret's mouth. Then she turned to the other little
girls.

"That will happen to anyone who dares to tell lies to
me. When you have cleaned out your mouth, Margaret,
you will go to bed without your supper."

Margaret took the dishrag from her mouth and flung it
into the sink.

"Thank you, I will go now, and anyway I wasn't want-
ing any supper."

Although Margaret stumped bravely up the stairs she

wasn't feeling brave inside for she knew that going to bed supperless would not be the end of her punishment.

When she had cleaned the taste of dishrag from her mouth with her toothbrush and was ready for bed, she found her tin box and hugged it to her.

"Oh, Hannah! Hannah!" she sobbed. "How am I to bear it? It gets worse here—not better."

But in the morning, as usually happens, things did look better. The sun was shining and even Matron could not prevent a child from going to school. And it was Margaret's favorite school day for in the afternoon there was dancing. They were learning a fan dance which, they were promised, the best six would dance at the end-of-term concert. It never crossed Margaret's mind that she might not be one of the six best.

The day was full of niceness. Miss Snelston was interested in their afternoon with Mr. Windle and a girl who had had a birthday on Saturday gave Margaret a little piece of her birthday cake.

Then it happened. The children were playing in the yard before afternoon classes. Margaret was skipping with some other girls who had a skipping rope when Miss Snelston called her.

"I have a job for you, dear." She held out some primroses. "One of the little ones picked these for me. Will you put them in water?"

Margaret ran into the schoolroom. It was empty except for Peter reading at his desk. She filled a pot with water from the tap behind the door, and arranging the primroses, put the pot on Miss Snelston's desk. Passing Peter on the way out, she gave the top of his head a friendly pat. He looked up, startled, and closed the book. Margaret saw the title—it was *Bleak House*. She snatched it up, and it opened at the flyleaf. There was a bookplate, though Margaret did not know that was what it was, and she could read clearly the name THOMAS AUGUSTUS WINDLE.

"Did you steal any more?" she asked Peter.

"I didn't steal them," Peter protested. "They're only borrowed. I'll give them back."

"How many did you take?"

Peter opened his desk. Inside, on top of *A Tale of Two Cities*, lay Sir Walter Scott's *Ivanhoe* and his *Kenilworth*. Feeling sick, Margaret opened both. As she expected, both belonged to Mr. Windle.

Margaret put *Bleak House* in the desk.

"Get a pencil and a piece of paper," she ordered Peter. He found a piece of drawing paper and a pencil.

"I only borrowed . . ." he started to say, but Margaret stopped him.

"Write this: 'Miss Snelston M'am will you see that these books which I borrowed get back to Mister Windle and oblige good-by Peter.' "

"Why good-by?" Peter asked. "I shall see her tomorrow."

Margaret shook her head.

"You leave that on top of the books after school. You won't see her any more for we have got to run away. It will have to be tonight before Mr. Windle finds the books are missing and sets the coppers on you."

Escape

Margaret felt as if a top were spinning inside her head. There were so many plans to make and so little time. In fact, it might be too late already if the police were at the orphanage.

To run away was one thing, but where should they run to? She could change her clothes, but Peter had nothing to change into so anyone who saw him would know where he came from. Then what about Horatio? Could they leave him alone in the orphanage?

By the time school was over Margaret had cleared her thoughts a little, but at the expense of her lessons— even of her beloved fan dance.

"What is the matter, dear?" Miss Snelston asked. "You've been very inattentive this afternoon, which is not like you. Are you tired after yesterday?"

Margaret longed to throw her arms around her and tell her everything but she believed she could not. If the police came for Peter it would be best if Miss Snelston knew nothing.

On the walk home Susan was puzzled at first because Margaret would not whisper to her as usual, but Margaret found an excuse.

"I'm in bad with Matron so I don't dare risk talking today."

It was on the walk home that Margaret found one answer to her problems—what to do with the two boys. She would take not only Peter but Horatio as well to Lavinia. On an enormous property like Sedgecombe Place there must be some place where Lavinia could hide the boys, and from what she had told them it would be easy to sneak out food to them. The next problem was how to find Sedgecombe Place.

"I know the thing to do is to get on the canal bank because there's that bit of the canal at the bottom of Mr. Windle's garden," she told herself, "and his garden is part of Sedgecombe Place. Then the only thing is to find Lavinia. Then when I've given her the boys I can go off by myself, which will be easy. Maybe I could get a place as a cook and when I do I'll write and tell Hannah and the rector where I am. I've still got two stamps inside my boot."

There were no police at the orphanage, Margaret was glad to see, but there was the usual difficulty in getting to speak to Peter. Margaret dared not risk being caught doing anything wrong for Matron would be sure to give her an extra bad punishment, perhaps locking her in a cupboard for hours. Tonight that would be a disaster. But after tea she had a little bit of luck. As it was a lovely evening twenty of the girls, including Margaret, were ordered to take what Matron grandly called "the linen" out and hang it on a line to air. It was while Margaret was doing this that she heard the big lawn mower and saw Peter—reading as usual—being the donkey, while his partner steered the mower.

A wave of temper swept over Margaret. Look at Peter, just reading a book as if nothing had happened while she was worrying herself sick about how to keep him out of prison! However, she had to speak to him and scolding him now would do no good. The important thing was to get him to Lavinia as quickly as possible and let her do the scolding.

"I must speak to Peter Beresford," she said to Susan, who was beside her. "If Matron comes out could you scream?"

"What about?" Susan asked.

Margaret, not for the first time, sighed at the dullness of Susan. If she had been the one asked to scream she could have thought of a dozen reasons.

"Say a wasp stung you."

Susan looked around.

"There aren't any wasps."

"Well, say you saw a mouse. You could, because there are outdoor mice as well as the indoor sort."

"I'll try," said Susan unwillingly. "But do be quick."

Margaret nodded and slipped behind bushes to the lawn Peter was helping to mow. He was so deep in his book he did not hear her so she clutched at his arm.

"Listen, and for goodness' sake do exactly what I tell you. Tonight, after Mr. Toms has gone to his room, roll under the beds, taking your clothes with you, until you get to Horatio's. Wake him up and, first getting his clothes, get him on the floor. Then both of you roll under the beds until you get to the last one. Then, if all is quiet, crawl out into the corridor. There you'll find me or if I'm not there wait for me. I shall be coming. It's quite easy rolling. I've done it before so I know."

"Where are we going?" Peter asked.

"To Lavinia. When she knows about your taking the books she'll hide you. She can't let you go to prison."

"Can you go to prison for borrowing books?"

"Mr. Windle won't think you borrowed, he'll think you stole. You can go to prison for less than that. Now go on, tell me what I've told you to do."

Peter seemed to have understood but then he said:

"What happens if I go to sleep before Mr. Toms shuts his door?"

That maddened Margaret.

"You really are a soppy boy. Here's me and Horatio running away all because of your beastly books and all you can say is"—she imitated him—" 'What happens if I go to sleep before Mr. Toms shuts his door?' "

Peter turned pink.

"I wasn't meaning it like that. Truly I am very grateful you are keeping me out of prison. I just meant how do you make yourself stay awake?"

"I don't know," said Margaret. "I just know I did it and if I can do it you can do it for we're the same age." She shut his book. "And don't read any more . . ." She broke off with a gasp for the book was *Bleak House*. "Oh, Peter! How could you! Now if we're caught you will have stolen property on you."

Peter turned his strange blue eyes on Margaret.

"You don't understand. I had finished *David Copperfield* and I have always wanted to read *Bleak House*. Mummy was trying to get a copy for me. If I have to go to prison I will think it worthwhile if I have read *Bleak House* first."

"And the other two?"

"I left them in my desk. I knew I couldn't run away with three books."

From the clothes line came a scream.

"I must go," Margaret said. "See you tonight with Horatio in the corridor outside your dormitory."

The scream from Susan was not a warning at the approach of Matron but came because the girls had finished hanging up the sheets and were going indoors.

"Thank you," Margaret whispered to Susan. "I would have been caught if you'd gone in without me. When nobody is looking sneak to my desk tomorrow. You'll find some sweets in a bag. Take them."

Sweets were so rare that Susan could not believe her ears.

"Take them! More than one do you mean?"

"Yes, take them all. You earned them. That was a good scream."

Margaret had no difficulty in staying awake. She still had a lot of planning to do. In fact, it came as a shock to her when she heard Miss Jones say "pray" and then, after the girls had scrambled up from their knees into their beds, "Good night, girls," as she wedged open the dormitory door before marching off to her bedroom.

When the time came to slip out of bed and leave the orphanage forever Margaret found she had a problem. Hannah's box, the tin box with a picture of a kitten on it which she had loved since she was a little girl. And Hannah had given it to her. How could she leave it in her bed to be taken by Matron? But rolling under beds by yourself was one thing and rolling with a tin box was another. So Margaret changed her plans. It would be easier and quicker to roll, but as she had her box she must crawl.

Afterwards Margaret never knew how she had done it for crawling in a long nightgown was difficult and crawling silently almost impossible. But somehow she succeeded and, stepping carefully over the board outside the dormitory which squeaked, was in the corridor on the way to the stairs which led up to the boys' dormitory.

Peter, though so dreamy-looking a boy, was very far from being stupid. After his time at the mowing machine was over he had hidden *Bleak House* where he could easily lay his hands on it in the dark and hurried into the orphanage to have a word with Horatio.

Although Margaret did not know it, Peter had managed a series of arrangements which gave him a chance to speak to his little brother. One was making himself responsible for Horatio's washing before and after meals. At such times the cloakrooms were always crowded so they couldn't say much, but seeing Horatio washed was one tiny link with the home they had once known. As usual, Peter found Horatio being cherished by two little girls in a game of "Home." He held out his hand.

"Come on. Wash time."

Horatio obediently joined Peter.

"That Emily," he confided, "is a very silly girl. She wants me to promise that when we play I will always be her little boy and belong to nobody else."

Peter drew Horatio into a corner outside the cloakroom door.

"Would you like to see Lavinia?"

Horatio beamed.

" 'Course I would. Where is she?"

Peter leaned down so Horatio could hear his whisper.

"This is a terribly important secret, and you mustn't tell anybody."

"I won't," said Horatio. "I know all about secrets."

"We're going to see her tonight."

Horatio was surprised.

"Doesn't Matron mind?"

"She doesn't know and she mustn't know. It's a secret between you, me and Margaret."

Horatio seemed suddenly much older than six.

"What do you want me to do?"

Peter put his mouth to Horatio's ear.

"You know after the beadle has said 'pray' how we get into bed as he turns the lights out?"

"I know," Horatio agreed.

"Do you think, just as the light goes out, instead of getting into bed you could get underneath it?"

"I could," Horatio agreed. "Then what do I do?"

"Nothing. Just wait there until I come for you. We have to get your clothes. Then we roll under the beds all the way to the door. Margaret says she will be in the corridor."

Horatio saw nothing to get excited about in these arrangements.

"I like rolling."

"Good," Peter said. "Now come and wash."

Everything went so easily as planned that it seemed strange to Margaret that all the orphans did not run away. She met the boys in the passageway and all crept down the two flights of stairs to the hall.

In the orphanage all the boots and shoes were cleaned as a before-breakfast task by boys who had earned a minor punishment. Overnight they were left downstairs by the orphans in rows in the passageway outside the kitchen. So before escaping the children had to find their boots. This was not easy in a dark passageway lined with ninety-seven other pairs. Margaret found hers by the stamps stuck inside the toe and Peter knew his by feel, but Horatio could not be sure his pair were his own. Anyway, they fitted and that was all that mattered. They escaped into the garden by the side door Margaret had used before.

Outside, it was Peter who took charge. Oddly enough, considering how vague he always seemed, he led the way to the shed where he had hidden Margaret's basket and his book as easily as if it were daylight, and he thought of things she might have forgotten.

"When Horatio and I have changed," he said, "what shall we do with our nightshirts?"

It was a dark night for the moon was behind a cloud. Margaret fumbled among her clothes. "I wish I could wear my lace," she thought, "but I can't because Hannah said Sunday and this is Monday." Aloud she said:

"By the time I've changed there could be room in my basket. I shan't take this awful old nightdress. I shall tie up a stone in it and sink it in the canal."

"I'd like that," Horatio said. "Peter, can I sink my nightshirt?"

"Better not," Peter decided. "It's all we've got to sleep in and Lavinia won't have any to give us."

It felt wonderful to Margaret to wear proper clothes again. She could not see herself but she could feel the liberty bodice, the scallops on the flannel petticoat, the featherstitching on the drawers and the crisp cambric of her petticoat. She had never been particularly attached to her pleated skirt and blue jersey, but it was nice to wear short skirts again and even nicer to be free. If she had not been afraid her boots would make a noise she would have skipped. "No more horrible meals," she thought. "No more Matron. No more Miss Jones. No more awful orphanage clothes."

Peter came across the shed to her. He and Horatio had changed so he was carrying their nightshirts.

"I should think you could get them into your basket because it's the sort that you can make bigger by doing up the strap loosely."

Margaret folded the nightshirts and put them and her tin box into the basket.

"We can take turns carrying it," Peter said, "for all I have is my book."

Margaret marveled that he could speak so calmly of stolen property. *His* book indeed! However, this was no time for quarreling. The sooner they were away from the orphanage the better.

"We better get started then for I don't know the way," she said.

Peter was surprised.

"Don't you? I do. We go down that lane before we get to the school and then across a field and there's the canal bank. Then we turn left and walk along it until we get to Mr. Windle's gate."

Margaret had taken it for granted that she would be the leader so for a second she was annoyed. Then she saw how silly that was as she didn't know the way and Peter did.

"All right," she said. "You lead. Come on, Horatio."

Jem

It was an eerie walk. The wind rustled last year's sedges on the canal bank, birds and animals let out strange little sounds, and once all three children nearly screamed when a cow put her head over a hedge to look at them. Peter had told Horatio they would pretend they were palefaces being chased by redskins so they must be as quiet as possible. But Horatio needed no game to help him to be quiet. Without a word he stumbled along behind Peter, grateful to know it was Margaret who was on his heels. Even the sinking of Margaret's nightdress was carried out in silence for Margaret merely rolled it around the biggest stone they could find and let it slide into the water.

Because they could not hurry in the dark it was over two hours before the children reached the little gate in Mr. Windle's wall which led to the canal bank. Margaret had been afraid they might miss it, but Peter knew what he was doing. He stopped suddenly.

"This is Mr. Windle's wall," he whispered. "If we go on to the end of the wall we come to the wood that is part

of Sedgecombe Place. There's a path if we could find it—
Lavinia said so."

Four miles is a long walk for a six-year-old, especially
in the middle of the night. In fact, it was a long walk for
them all.

"Before we go into the wood," Margaret suggested,
"couldn't we sit down for a little? Horatio is tired."

Horatio was not having that. "I'm only a little bit
tired. I can still walk for hours and hours."

Peter, whose turn it had been to carry the basket, gave
it to Margaret.

"You two wait here while I find the path. Lavinia said
it led straight to the house. Do you know where she
sleeps?"

Margaret felt along the bank for a comfortable place to
sit down.

"No, but Jem will. We have to find the stables. His is
the last room and it has a horseshoe over the door."

"Right," said Peter. "You can find him. Now wait
here. I shan't be long finding the path."

The uniform cloaks were hung up in the cloakroom at
the orphanage so the boys had not brought them with
them. When they sat down Margaret noticed that it was
cold. She wished that somehow she had managed to get
her coat out. She put an arm around Horatio.

"Let's keep each other warm until Peter gets back."

"Let's," said Horatio, and immediately went to sleep.
One minute later so did Margaret.

They were awakened by Peter's shaking them.

"Come on. I've not only found the path but also where
the stables are. Follow me."

Because they had been asleep neither Margaret nor

Horatio had noticed how long Peter had been away. So
they were surprised as they followed him through the
wood to find what a distance it was to the house and
stables. But at last Peter stopped.

"This path on the right leads to the stables," he whispered. "They are cobbled so we'd better not all go in
because of noise. You go, Margaret, but you had better
leave your boots here."

Margaret was not nearly as good as Peter at finding her
way about in the dark. "The last bedroom over the
stables," Jem had said. It was easy to tell she was in the
stables for there was a nice horse smell and an occasional

small stamping as a horse moved in its sleep. But where were the staff's bedrooms? The horses' stalls were on both sides so which was the last? Then quite by accident she found something. Her hand touched some steps which led upward above the horses' stalls.

Her heart in her mouth lest she make a noise, Margaret climbed the steps and found herself on what seemed to be a landing. There was no question she had reached the grooms' bedrooms for from behind each door—and there seemed to be four of them—came shattering snores. Carefully Margaret felt her way along to the end, then lifted her hands to the top of the door. At first she thought she was outside the wrong room. Then her fingers felt cold metal—it was Jem's horseshoe. The door was fastened by a latch. Softly and slowly she lifted it.

Jem was dreaming he was riding the winner of the Grand National when he felt a hand on his face and heard a whisper.

"Wake up, Jem. Wake up. It's me—Margaret."

Jem had been used most of his life to being awakened at unexpected moments. On the canal all types of emergencies could occur so his father had expected all his children to spring out of their sleep at a shout. But this was different. Margaret? Who was Margaret?

"What d'you want?" he asked. "Who are you?"

Margaret patted what she guessed would be Jem's shoulder under the blanket.

"You remember. You fetched me and Peter and Horatio from the orphanage."

With a sinking heart Jem did remember.

"To take you to Mr. Windle's. You 'aven't run away, 'ave you?"

Margaret sat on the bed while in a whisper she poured out her story.

"So you see we simply had to get away. I couldn't let them put Peter in prison."

Jem had an inborn fear of the police. Since he was a baby his father had threatened that if he did this or that the coppers would have him, so he accepted without question the idea that Peter had to be hidden.

"But what can I do? I couldn't 'ide a cat, not in these parts."

Margaret settled more comfortably on the bed.

"I don't want you to do anything. All I want is for you to go into the house and fetch Lavinia."

Margaret had been going to say more but Jem was so shocked at her suggestion of fetching Lavinia that he bounced up in bed so violently he nearly threw her onto the floor.

"Inside the 'ouse! Me! I ain't never been inside since I 'ad pneumonia. If I was caught inside it'd be me what the coppers are after."

Margaret saw her whole plan falling in ruins.

"But you must go inside sometimes. Where do you eat?"

"One of the groom's wives does for us and a right good cook she is."

"So you truthfully don't know where Lavinia sleeps? Now what shall I do? I suppose we had better wait outside the kitchen until she gets up in the morning. I suppose you can show us where the kitchen is?"

Jem was appalled. He was happy working in the stables and now, thanks to this orphan, he could see himself being dismissed without a character reference.

He could imagine the questions there would be if Margaret and the two boys were found outside the kitchen in the morning, and he had no doubt that it would soon be known that Margaret had been to his room. He shivered with fright.

"You can't sit outside the kitchen door. Proper state everyone will be in."

"It's what I'm going to do," said Margaret. "I can't hide the boys. For one thing they are dressed in the orphanage uniform and you know what that looks like."

Jem had to agree to that.

"Proper figures of fun."

"So if you can't show me which is the kitchen someone else will have to. Who sleeps in the next room?"

Jem leaned forward in the bed and clutched at where he supposed Margaret was sitting. He caught her by the arm.

"Oh no! You dursent do that. You'll get me the sack, true as life you will. I tell you straight, if you wake up the other lads they'll rouse the 'ouse and that'll bring the coppers 'ere as quick as their bicycles will bring them."

"Well, then, what am I to do?"

Margaret was desperate and this showed in her voice. It matched the desperation Jem was feeling.

"Now sit quiet-like while I think. You can't go to the 'ouse an' that's flat so we got to think of somethin' else."

"What else?"

Slowly—for nothing came quickly to Jem—an idea was being born.

"Quiet now, lass." Then, after a pause: "And it might work too, it might an' all."

Margaret hated to be kept waiting.

"What might?"

Jem had his idea clear now.

"My dad's boat is tied up two miles up the canal. So I see'd 'em tonight. When I left my brother, young Tom, he steps a bit of the way along of me. 'E says 'e's 'ad it, 'e won't leg the 'orses no more. 'E said 'e was runnin' away."

Margaret leaped ahead of Jem.

"You mean Peter could leg instead of Tom?"

"That's the idea."

"But what about me and Horatio?"

Now Jem had a plan he was keen to carry it out.

"You nip along back to the boys. Stay in the bushes outside the stable entrance. When I come back I'll give a whistle."

"But what about me and Horatio?" Margaret asked again. "Now that we've run away we'll have to stay away. Matron would kill us if we went back."

Jem was tired of questions.

"You nip along. I'm 'avin' a word with me ma. Shouldn't wonder if she'll manage with the lot of you. Powerful fond of our Tom our ma is. Do a lot, she would, to give 'im 'is chance to get away."

Polly Makes a Discovery

So scared were the orphans of being blamed for something they had not done that none of the children mentioned that Margaret, Peter and Horatio were missing. But in the girls' dormitory Miss Jones, counting heads before the children were marched down to breakfast, missed Margaret, and in the boys' dormitory Ben, expecting to wash Horatio, spotted he was not there and this led to the fact that Peter was also missing.

In the memory of Winifred, who had been under the orphanage roof longer than any of the other children, there had not been a morning like it. It was rumored afterward that Miss Jones screamed all the way to Matron's office. The boys swore that Ben had rushed into Mr. Toms's room without knocking and so caught him still in bed. But whatever the truth, it was certain that the orphanage was shaken from head to foot. So shaken that Mary and Winifred were called in to serve the breakfast and, forgetting the rules in all the excitement, tipped each porridge plate full of milk and slammed down plates of bread on the tables and told the children to help themselves. As a result the children went to school better fed than they had ever been before.

When the orphans were lined up ready to march to school Matron came out of her office. Her face was no longer red but a sort of greeny-yellow, and her upholstered chest inside her black dress was heaving as if she had run upstairs.

"You will have heard that Margaret Thursday and the Beresford boys are missing. This matter is being dealt with by the police, who will no doubt bring the culprits back within an hour." She paused there. "I need not tell you that the runaways will be very severely punished." The children shivered. "And should there prove to be a ringleader"—again Matron paused and all the children thought "Margaret"—"there will be such punishment as will be remembered as long as this orphanage stands. Now this is an order. There is to be no mention at school that Margaret, Peter and Horatio are missing. The matter will be handled by the police and I do not want talk in the village. I have my ways of finding out if any one of you children disobey me and I can promise you that if I am disobeyed the offender will spend the whole evening locked in the understairs cupboard and then go supperless to bed. You may go now. Quick. March."

Matron's words were taken to heart by even the smallest orphans so nothing was said about Margaret, Peter and Horatio. But Miss Jones spoke to Miss Snelston about their absence.

"They have a slight rash so Matron has kept them at

home. Probably due to overeating at Mr. Windle's on Sunday."

Miss Snelston received this news with misgiving. In the past both she and Polly had cared for orphans who had been marched to school when so ill that the proper place for them was bed. So it was strange to hear of three children being kept away for a slight rash.

"I don't like the sound of it," Miss Snelston told Polly. "I suspect we're in for an epidemic of something. Matron would never keep those children at home for an ordinary rash."

It turned out to be an unusual morning in another way for after the children had gone home to their dinners the Countess of Corkberry's carriage drove up to the school gate.

Polly was just laying out her own and Miss Snelston's lunch when the Countess walked into the schoolroom.

"Oh dear!" she said, looking at the food. "I've come at a bad moment."

Miss Snelston gave Polly a look to tell her to clear away the lunch and offered the Countess a chair.

"Not a bad moment at all. We only have something light and cold. Our main meal is in the evening."

Polly carried the lunch into the other schoolroom. The Countess waited until she had shut the door.

"I am the Countess of Corkberry," the Countess explained, "and I have called on you at this time because I knew the orphans would be absent. I have a girl from the orphanage working in my scullery—or rather she has two brothers at the orphanage. She has said nothing but I and some of my senior staff have the impression that she feels the boys do not get enough to eat. In fact, the younger

boy, Horatio, described the menu and it did sound inadequate. I realize, of course, that children often complain
about food without cause, but I must admit I feel disturbed."

Miss Snelston had sometimes dreamed of something
like this happening. Someone influential—someone who
cared—looking into the affairs of the orphanage. She was
so thankful to see Lady Corkberry she could—had she
dared—have kissed her.

"Oh, Lady Corkberry, I cannot tell you how glad I am
you have come to me. I have been at this school now for
five years and never a day but I have worried about those
orphans." Lady Corkberry was puzzled.

"But if that is the case why could you not go to the
ladies' committee or talk to one of the governors?"

"None of the ladies on the committee belong to this

village—I do not even know their names. The women here say that the ladies' committee have dust thrown in their eyes by the matron. I am afraid she is a hard woman. Many of my children come to school with their hands badly scarred through beatings and I suspect they are scarred in other places too."

"And the children are hungry?"

"Always, I fear. We do what we can and so do the village mothers. They often send an extra apple and sometimes a cake. But you know how it is. Times are hard for farm laborers so what food there is they need for themselves, and schoolteachers are not well paid."

Lady Corkberry nodded sympathetically.

"I understood from Horatio that Polly Jenkin fed him."

Miss Snelston looked toward the other room. She spoke apologetically.

"She is my little assistant and was an orphan herself so she knows what it is like. Horatio is a dear little boy and nicely spoken. Of course, it's not fair to help one child and not another but, you see, there are one hundred orphans."

"I do indeed see." Lady Corkberry got up. "I must not keep you any longer from your luncheon, but I can promise you I will somehow look thoroughly into affairs at the orphanage and see that what is wrong is put right."

Miss Snelston also got up.

"I feel you must wonder why I have done nothing though suspecting so much. But apart from knowing nobody on the committee, interference from me might easily have caused my dismissal and I should regret that, for at least I know the orphans are happy while under my care and I think perhaps I give them all the love they have ever known."

Lady Corkberry held out her hand.

"Good-by. I am sure of that. And please don't blame yourself. It is people like myself who have the means and the time to help but who passed by on the other side. It is we who are to blame."

Polly, her eyes goggling with interest, came back with the lunch as soon as she heard Lady Corkberry drive away.

"That was the Countess, wasn't it? Such a lovely carriage—I saw it from the window."

"Yes, she does a lot of good work, but she doesn't often come this way for this isn't Corkberry land. I have seen her several times, though, and once I went to Sedgecombe Place when they threw the grounds open—it was some political affair and I went along with one of the farmers and his wife."

Polly helped herself to a sandwich.

"What did she want?"

Miss Snelston longed to confide in Polly but she didn't dare. There would be enough talk about Lady Corkberry's calling as it was. She thought quickly for an explanation which would satisfy not only Polly but the whole village.

"She is interested in a charity. Maybe when the summer comes there will be a fete or something and our children might do some dancing."

Polly glowed.

"Wouldn't that be fun! That maypole dance is ever so pretty."

Miss Snelston wanted to change the subject. She

looked down the classroom. On each desk but two lay
scrubbed slates ready for the afternoon's work. Her eyes
fell upon Peter's desk.

"I wonder what Peter keeps in his desk. It doesn't shut
properly."

"I'll look," said Polly. "I expect it's that book he's always reading—*A Tale of Two Cities*. He says it's exciting so I'm going to read it when he's through." She had
reached Peter's desk and threw it open. After a pause she
came back holding Peter's note and the two books. She
gave the note to Miss Snelston.

" 'Will you see these books . . .' " Miss Snelston read
out loud, then she broke off. "Why does he say 'Good-
by'?"

Polly looked blank.

"I don't know. That's funny. He couldn't have known
he was going to have a rash."

Miss Snelston had turned quite pale.

"It's more than funny. Oh, Polly, where are Peter,
Margaret and Horatio? I have a feeling something is very
wrong."

The Nightdress

The stone Margaret had found was not big enough or securely enough fastened to the nightdress to cause it to sink for long. At some time during the night it had got free and had risen from the bottom of the canal to get tangled in some of last year's reeds. Ordinarily it would have clung there unnoticed unless one of the canal women had seen it and pulled it on board hoping to make use of it. But that morning, as soon as the children had left for school, the beadle had been sent hurrying to fetch the local policeman.

Police Constable Perkins was a rather slow man. There was almost no crime in the village for him to bother about except on days when there was a fair in the neighborhood, when there might be a few drunks about and maybe a fight or two. So mostly life was easy. In fact, the village usually saw their policeman bent over his kitchen garden, where he grew onions which were the admiration of all. So it was in his kitchen garden that the beadle found him when he panted up to his gate.

"Matron up at the orphanage wants to see you immediate," he gasped, for he was unused to running.

"What's up then?" Perkins asked.

Mr. Toms was not giving anything away.

"You'll know soon enough and you better 'urry."

So Police Constable Perkins put on his uniform jacket, clipped his trouser legs, mounted his bicycle and rode off to the orphanage.

Like most of the villagers, Police Constable Perkins was scared of Matron, so scared that he had never encouraged local gossip about the orphanage.

"Now, now," he would say when one of the village women would hint things weren't right. "There's a committee of ladies looks after that place and if they are satisfied reckon we should be. It's not for us to criticize what's done by our betters."

Matron saw Perkins in her office.

"How the children got out of their dormitories I cannot imagine. The escape from the house is quite clear —a side door has been found open. I have no doubt at all where they have gone. The sister of the two boys works in Sedgecombe Place so all three are almost certainly with her."

Perkins was writing all this down. He stopped when Matron mentioned Sedgecombe Place.

"Sedgecombe Place isn't rightly on my beat. I should 'ave to pass that on to the police constable in Sedgecombe village."

"Don't talk nonsense!" Matron snapped. "This orphanage is on your beat. All you have to do is go to Sedgecombe Place and ask to see the scullery maid. Her name is Lavinia Beresford. I will spell that for you. Demand from her where she has hidden the children, then bring them back here to me."

Perkins wrote everything down.

"Would I ask her ladyship if I could see the young woman Beresford?"

Matron struggled to control her temper.

"Of course not. You will go to the back door and ask to see the girl. I do not anticipate that you will have any difficulty with her. It is likely she will be thankful to hand back the children for she knows they have a good home here and how happy they have been. Do not tell anyone except the girl why you are there. The fewer people who know about this the better."

Police Constable Perkins got back on his bicycle and, via a footpath across a field, reached the canal bank. There he rode slowly along thinking not of missing orphans but of summer days and fishing.

The nightdress was hanging on the reeds at a place where two summers ago he had caught a monster carp and Perkins chanced to see it. He got off his bicycle, leaned against the hedge and carefully, for the bank was slippery, hauled in the nightdress. It was an unattractive sight, soaked in water and stained with mud, so that he would probably have thrown it back if he had not seen on the inside of the neck in large ink letters st. luke's orphanage.

"Oh my! Oh my!" he murmured. " 'Just go to the back door,' she said, but this is more than that. This is a great deal more than that. This is a dredging matter."

He rolled up the nightdress, tied it to his handlebars, got back on his bicycle and, peddling furiously this time, rode not to Sedgecombe Place but to Police Constable Frinton's cottage in Sedgecombe village. He was peddling so hard and his head was so full of what he had to tell Constable Frinton that he scarcely saw a canal boat called *The Crusader* gliding by, and though he had to wait to let it pass he paid no attention to a small boy who was leading a horse, even though the small boy was attempting to read a book at the same time.

Although telephones had been invented, very few houses in the country areas had them so news did not reach people in a few seconds. But that did not mean that news did not get around, so the first person who saw Constable Frinton and Constable Perkins set off to the canal carrying waders and pitchforks rushed around Sedgecombe village spreading the news.

"Someone's drownded in the canal. Must be over t'other side for t'was Constable Perkins who came to fetch Constable Frinton."

Of course the gossip reached Sedgecombe Place. It came via one of the stable lads who had taken a horse to the blacksmith.

"Someone's drownded in the canal," he told those in the stable.

"Someone's drownded in the canal," one of the grooms told a gardener.

"Someone's drownded in the canal," the gardener told Mrs. Smedley when he brought in the house vegetables.

"Hear that, girls?" Mrs. Smedley called out. "Someone's drowned themselves in the canal, poor soul."

Lavinia, scrubbing potatoes at the sink, said to Clara:

"Who would do a thing like that? I'm glad it didn't happen on my Sunday off. I would hate to see the poor soul do it."

The only person who took the news personally was Jem. Margaret had told him she had got rid of her nightdress in the canal. Immediately he heard someone was supposed to be drowned he put two and two together and came out in a cold sweat. That silly girl! If the police thought someone was drowned it wouldn't be just a matter of three orphans missing, which wouldn't have caused much concern, but a real thorough search would be made. A big search was almost certain to include the canal boats, and if it did could his mother, smart as she was, hide three children she couldn't account for?

"Oh dear!" worried Jem. "I wish I'd never set eyes on young Margaret. She'll get me the sack yet. I know she will."

Meanwhile the news was spreading to Constable Perkins's own village, but now with more detail. For in spite of Matron's strictures the news had leaked out that three orphans were missing. So the moment it was known that the constables were raking up the bottom of the canal the village put two and two together. Doors were flung open and the women gathered in knots.

"Those poor little children drownded."

"Nor I don't wonder. Beaten black and blue, shouldn't be surprised. That matron ought to be behind bars, that's where she oughter be."

"Rough musicking that's what her needs."

"And that's what her is going to get this very night."

Rough music, as it was called, was a country way of expressing public disapproval. After it was dark the whole village would turn out to beat on pots, kettles, anything that would make a noise. Then they would form a procession and march for perhaps two hours around the offender's cottage. It was an effective punishment for ill-doers for the noise carried for miles, so the next day

"Who was rough-musicked last night?" was the question on everybody's lips. As a rule shame brought the offenders to their senses. To rough-music Matron would serve a double purpose, for it would not only bring shame on her but was an immensely effective way of seeing that attention was focused on the orphanage.

At the orphanage Matron was almost frantic with worry. Of course the news had been brought to her that the police were dredging the canal, and close on top of that someone had passed on the news that Lady Corkberry had called at the school. Ever since Matron had been at the orphanage she had been dishonestly squeezing a little money here and a little money there so that she could have a nest-egg for her retirement. Was everything to be lost because of three worthless orphans? "If Margaret were to come in now," she told herself, "I could strangle her with my bare hands." Then worse thoughts came. Suppose, just suppose the children were drowned. Would matters finish there? Would local ladies like Lady Corkberry poke in their noses and start asking questions?

It was the longest day Matron had ever known. She sent the beadle to Police Constable Perkins to find out if he had any news, but he was out. His wife who, with the rest of the village was against Matron, would only say:

"You tell 'er there's no news and Mr. Perkins 'e wouldn't wonder if this time no news was bad news."

It was just after the orphans had gone to bed that the rough musicking started. The men, when they came in from work, had been solidly behind their womenfolk.

"Bin talk about that old orphanage since that matron come."

"Time she was taught a lesson."

"Doan't want no more orphans trying to drownded theirselves."

So as soon as it was dark the village went to the orphanage and the noise started. Matron went to her window, drew aside the curtain and peered out. It was a frightening sight for the villagers were angry. There was moonlight and by it she could see the expressions on their faces as they beat on their pots and pans. The noise rose and rose and was accompanied by an angry murmur. Matron lost her head. She dropped the curtain and ran from wall to wall beating against them as if she were a moth trapped by a light. As she ran she moaned:

"Oh no! Don't let them in. They'll kill me. I know they'll kill me."

When at last the rough music finished Matron was unconscious on the floor.

Ma Smith

Jem was lucky that the night he had to see his mother the boat was tied up for it did not happen every trip. It was quite usual for his father, the captain, as all owners of canal boats are called, to make a straight trip to London without a stop. Each trip took ten days and it was quite commonplace during those ten days for neither the captain nor his wife to rest long enough to take their clothes off. So on many a trip Jem's only chance to see his family was when they were going through a lock. The reason for the tie-up that night was that the boat needed a minor repair.

Jem's mother had not yet gone to bed when he crept back on board. She was in the galley boiling a kettle of water so that there would be a cup of tea ready for her husband when he finished work. She was startled when Jem came in.

"Our Jem! What's brought you back this time of night?"

Jem jerked his head aft toward the cabin where Tom was sleeping.

"Young Tom stepped along of me after I left 'ere. Ma, 'e won't be a legger no more. 'E'll run away."

His mother nodded.

"I knew it was comin'. Each day I thank Gawd when I find 'e's still 'ere of a mornin'."

" 'E wants to live along of Bert," Jem said.

Bert was the brother who had run away from working on the canal. He had made friends with another young man and together they owned a quite prosperous rag-and-bone business in Wolverhampton.

" 'Tisn't the rag-and-bone business," his mother told Jem. "It's the schoolin'. The captain give 'im his two-pence a week regular for the school each end of a trip and I send 'im lookin' ever so nice with 'is slate on 'is back. But that ain't enough, for our Tom wants to go every day. Well, our Bert 'e says Tom oughter 'ave 'is chance and 'e can live along of 'im and go to school."

"But you can't manage without 'im."

His mother fixed her large dark eyes on Jem.

" 'Ow can we? That Ebeneezer we 'ave to 'elp the captain 'asn't got no more brains than a sparrer. I done what I could—many's the night I been the legger while Tom got a sleep. An' so 'e should, a growin' boy like 'im."

Jem moved nearer to his mother. He lowered his voice.

"Listen, Mum. I think I've found a way around things."

Out poured the story Margaret had told him, repeated as far as he could remember in Margaret's own words. When he had finished he stood quietly watching his mother's face. There was a candle and by its light he could see her thoughts racing across it like cloud shadows across a field of corn. At last she said:

"Is the boy what the coppers are after dark like our Tom?"

"No. 'Air the color of barley 'e 'as but you could fix 'im up to be dark."

His mother gave a slight bow of the head to show she accepted that.

"And the young boy, is 'e tough? For 'e'll need to be a legger too. Why Tom 'e couldn't manage on 'is own so a green young 'un couldn't."

Jem could tell that his mother was going to accept the children.

"I'll fetch 'em. Should be back 'ere in less than an 'our."

His mother held up a warning finger.

"When you get back listen for the captain snoring before you come on the boat. I shall say nothin' to 'im tonight. When we start tomorrer Tom will 'ave gone and the other kids will be 'ere. It'll be easier that way. Creep up on 'im sort of."

When about three-quarters of an hour later Jem and the children arrived on the bank beside the boat there was no need to listen for the captain's snores. They reverberated like thunder along the canal bank. Jem made a sign to the children to stay where they were while he crept quietly on board.

Jem's mother decided it would be safer if she came

ashore to meet the children for any noise on board might wake the captain.

Margaret was never to forget her first sight of Jem's mother. She loomed up out of the night so enormous a woman it was as if a huge animal were standing beside her. She carried a lantern so by its light Margaret was able to see more or less what she looked like: the mass of dark hair with a trilby hat on top of it tied under her chin by a scarf; the wide voluminous black dress; the vivid colored shawl which was around her shoulders.

"I'm Mrs. Smith, Jem's ma," the woman explained. "You'll 'ear me called Ma Smith up and down the canal but to you I am Mrs. Smith."

"Yes, ma'am," Peter and Margaret had said together.

Horatio was almost asleep so he had not answered.

"I don't want no ma'ams," Mrs. Smith said firmly. "We're plain canal folk what don't believe in airs and graces." She moved the lantern so the light fell on Peter. "'E don't look the cut of a gaol bird to me," she said to Jem. "You better take 'im on the boat and do something with 'is face and 'air if 'e's to pass for our Tom. There's some walnut juice top shelf in the galley and I've put out on the table that black dye what I bought at Lostock Fair." She swung the lantern over to Margaret. "I meant to use it for meself where I'm goin' gray but I've never got around to it. You come with me, girl. I'll 'ave to cut your 'air off and fix you up in togs of our Tom's for you'll 'ave to be the legger when we start, for 'is"—she looked at Peter—"'air won't be dry. You better fetch our Tom, Jem, and tell 'im 'e can go. We 'aven't long for the captain wants to start real early, which is good for it'll be dark so 'e won't see who is legging, 'an by the time the sun's up the boy can 'ave took over as legger and I'll 'ave told the captain what's been arranged."

Mrs. Smith took Margaret to the galley. There she sat her down and with large scissors chopped off her hair.

"Pity," she said. "Lovely 'air, but there it is. From the cut of 'im that boy won't 'ave the strength of our Tom so you'll 'ave to 'elp out. Time I've put some walnut on your face and togged you out in Tom's clothes you'll pass for a boy anywhere."

"Has Tom lots of clothes?" Margaret asked. "Because Peter and Horatio will need clothes too. I expect you couldn't see in the dark, but they've got on their orphanage uniforms which are very queer."

"I saw," Mrs. Smith said. "We'll manage. Throw

nothin' away has always been my motto. Comes in 'andy at times like now.''

Mrs. Smith was daubing Margaret's face with walnut juice when Tom came to the galley. Margaret couldn't see him for he was behind her and Mrs. Smith did not pause in her daubing.

"You off, Son?"

"Yes, Ma."

"Come and see us next time we're passing Wolver-hampton."

" 'Course," Tom agreed and then apparently was gone for he said no more.

Mrs. Smith said no more either. Then, sounding rather as if she had a cold, she fumbled in her pocket.

"It's the walnut juice," she said. "Makes me eyes water."

Soon afterward Mrs. Smith led Margaret to a small cabin. It had several bunks in it, on one of which Horatio was asleep.

"This is the for'ard cabin," Mrs. Smith explained. "Ebeneezer—'e's the hired man—'e slept aft along of Tom. You better doss down quick for it won't be long now before the captain wants to start."

To Margaret it seemed not more than five minutes before Mrs. Smith had shaken her awake.

"Come on, dearie. Put on these clothes."

The clothes were a pair of dark trousers, a knitted jersey and a battered old soft hat.

Margaret had not undressed before going to bed so she undressed now.

"Shall I keep on my bodice?" she asked. "The suspenders will keep my stockings up."

Mrs. Smith was folding the clothes Margaret had taken off.

"No, you can't wear no stockings nor socks neither. The men and boys on the canal boats never do. Just your boots. Cruel 'ard it'll be at first but you'll get used to it." She stroked Margaret's petticoat. "My, they dressed you fine at that orphanage. Lovely work this is."

Margaret nearly burst with rage.

"Those clothes aren't orphanage clothes, they're mine, and there's more in that basket, one set with real lace. If we hadn't run away Matron was going to steal my clothes."

Mrs. Smith kept her mind on the business in hand.

"You tuck the jersey into the trousers and put this belt around." Then she looked at Margaret's basket. "We'll keep you dressed as a boy for the time bein' so I'll pack this stuff away. Now come on, I'll show you 'ow to 'arness the 'orse."

Margaret had seen nothing of a horse.

"Where is he?"

"Tied up down the bank. Reckon it's one of the best nights the poor old fellow ever 'ad. 'Owever 'ard you 'ave to work on this boat, Margaret, you remind yourself the 'orse works 'arder."

Wilberforce

Jem was no actor so on the day the children escaped he had found life hard in the stables. Rumors had flown around like bees about to swarm. Jem had been expected not only to react to each rumor but also to gossip about it with the other lads.

"They say the matron pushed them into the canal and drownded them." "Three little 'uns is missin'." "Mr. Frinton and Mr. Perkins is dredging for them now."

A quick calculation told Jem *The Crusader* should be safely past the dredging operations. Knowing where the children were, it was hard to sound horrified. He leaned down to pick up a piece of cleaning leather.

"Did oughter be 'orse whipped that matron," another lad said, "or maybe 'anged."

Later there was more news relayed by the postman.

"The police constable couldn't find the bodies. They say they are going to ask for help from Scotland Yard. Just imagine that now! Never had Scotland Yard here before."

Then came the rumors as to where the children had been seen. In Wolverhampton. On trains. In a carrier's cart. In a gypsy encampment.

"Not a mention of *The Crusader*," thought Jem thankfully and, because he was so thankful, he managed suitable replies.

"Well I never!" "Gone to Wolverhampton!" "So the gypsies got 'em!" "Mr. Frinton will soon 'ave them back then."

From the stable point of view the most startling news came, via his valet, from Lord Corkberry.

"We're going to Ireland," the valet said to the head coachman. "Stayin' with the Marquis of Delaware."

The head coachman and the valet were old friends.

"Now!" said the head coachman. "Whatever for? There's no huntin' now."

The valet tapped the side of his nose in a meaning way.

"I think there's more in these missing orphans than meets the eye. If you ask me it's mixed up some way with Ireland. Anyway we leave tomorrow. You're driving us to the boat in the carriage."

Off went the head coachman to give his orders. The carriage, which was spotless, was to be brought out and polished. The harness for the horses was to shine like diamonds.

"His lordship," the head coachman confided to the second coachman, "is leavin' for Ireland. I'm driving him to the coast in the carriage."

That was like putting a match to dry bracken. The rumors flew out of the stable all over the estate to the village.

"The orphans have been seen in Ireland. His lordship is going himself to fetch them back."

Jem felt wretched. He had been forced to refuse Margaret's request to give Lavinia a message to say the boys were safe. He knew Margaret had not understood that in his position there was no excuse for him to go near the house. And if he ran into Lavinia in the grounds, as he sometimes did, given a message like that who knew what a girl might do? Screech out or faint dead away, most like. And one thing was certain sure, when it was known it was he who had given Lavinia the message they would have the truth out of him in the swish of a cow's tail, and that would mean the rozzers on board *The Crusader,* which would not only bring terrible trouble on his ma and dad but would be the end of his fine job in the stables.

However, Jem was a good-hearted boy, so though unwilling he had allowed Peter to write a note. They had no proper paper but they found a small piece in which sweets had been wrapped and there was a stub of pencil in Peter's pocket. Peter had written: "Dear Lavinia we are with Margaret and quite safe do not show this to anyone love Peter and Horatio." He had folded this over and written "Miss Lavinia Beresford" on the back.

"I'm not makin' no promises, mind," Jem had said as he put the note in a pocket. "I can't give it to Lavinia but if I can find somewhere to leave it so someone else picks it up and gives it to her then I will."

The wilder the rumors got the more that note from Peter weighed in Jem's pocket. What had Lavinia heard? Did she believe the boys were drowned? Was she crying her eyes out?

Then after his dinner Jem got some real news. It came from Clara, with whom Lavinia shared a bedroom. She had awakened that morning with a raging toothache so Mrs. Tanner, hearing that all normal remedies had been of no avail, ordered the trap to be brought around to take Clara to the dentist. Jem was told to drive it.

On the outward journey Clara had said nothing, clasping a woolen shawl to her face and groaning. But on the return journey, free from pain for the tooth had been removed, she was full of talk.

"Nobody hasn't been allowed to tell Lavinia, not yet. That was an order from her ladyship herself."

"I suppose Lavinia will be upset when they do tell her," Jem had suggested.

Clara had swung round to gape at him.

"Upset! With two brothers drownded or worse! Why, those brothers are all she thinks about. I reckon when she knows she'll go stark starin' mad."

Having delivered Clara to the back door, Jem drove the trap back to the stable and, being free, after he had stabled the horse and helped put away the trap, went up to his room and sat down to do something he rarely did—think.

Where in the whole of Sedgecombe Place could you put a note someone was certain to find? Dozens of ideas went through his head but none of them made sense. Then, as if given to him as a sign, a dog barked.

Sedgecombe Place was full of dogs. There were four retrievers for the shooting, and they lived with the head keeper. Two puppy hounds lived in the stables. A spotted dog which ran under the dogcart was looked after by the gardener. There were also several house dogs, includ-

ing a small white fluffy dog which belonged to Lady
Corkberry. This dog was supposed to stay in the house
but, though small, it had the courage of a lion and would
roam where its fancy took it, including into the stables,
which is where Jem had met it. It was the business of one
of the footmen each afternoon to find the dog and take it
back to the house at teatime. The dog's name was Wilberforce—it was given a lot of other names by the staff,
none of which were polite. Now Jem knew who should
carry Peter's note—it was Wilberforce.

Well fed though he was, Wilberforce was fond of a
snack of garbage. There was a splendid garbage heap at
the end of the kitchen garden ready to be burned in an
incinerator. Strolling casually as if admiring the vegetables, Jem walked through the kitchen garden. He was in
luck, for the gardeners were pricking out seedlings in the
greenhouses so there was no one about. Gingerly, Jem
walked toward the garbage heap. Would Wilberforce
have chosen somewhere else to go that afternoon? Then
Jem's heart leaped. Sticking out of the rubbish heap was
a wagging tail attached to something white.

It was a quick job. Jem picked up Wilberforce. Then,
talking to him gently to prevent him from yapping, he
tied the note securely to his soft pale blue collar.

"Now you be careful," he said as he put Wilberforce
down. "It would be ever so easy to tear that bit of paper
off you."

Then, as secretly as he had come, Jem slipped out of
the kitchen garden.

When Lord Corkberry joined Lady Corkberry for tea
half an hour later, the butler came in carrying Wilberforce.

"M'lady, Henry fetched Wilberforce, as he always does, from the garden—or rather, I would gather from the odor, from the garbage heap—and he saw this hanging from his collar."

"This" was Peter's note, now terribly dirty and torn.

Lord Corkberry laughed.

"Been gettin' love letters, old man?" he asked Wilberforce.

The butler held the grimy note away from him as if it would bite.

"It is addressed, m'lord, to the young woman in the scullery whose brothers are missing from the orphanage."

Lord Corkberry held out a hand.

"Is it, by jove!" He took the note and turned it over. "That's right. Now what do we do? If it's bad news don't like just to shove the note at the girl."

The butler cleared his throat.

"It is not sealed, m'lord, just folded."

Lord Corkberry gave him a shrewd glance.

"So Henry had a look and I daresay you did too."

Lady Corkberry broke in.

"I think we must read it for if it's bad news the shock might make the child ill." She turned to the butler. "Ask Mrs. Smedley to be so good as to send Lavinia Beresford up here immediately."

The captain found Peter and Horatio a glorious joke. Mrs. Smith, choosing a moment when there was no one about either on land or on the water, brought them to meet her husband, who was steering the boat. She had done what she could to change the boys' appearance but the dye for their hair had come out wrong. What promised on the bottle to restore graying hair to its original rich chestnut had turned Peter and Horatio's fair hair a strange dark green. Their far too pale faces for canal boys had been daubed with walnut juice, but it had not gone on smoothly all over so they had a mottled look. Since they could not wear their orphanage clothes, Mrs. Smith had dug out of a chest clothes that had belonged to her sons when they were small. Evidently at all ages the Smith boys had been far broader than Peter and Horatio for the clothes hung on them in folds which, together with their green hair, gave them an odd scarecrow look.

"These are the boys," Mrs. Smith said. "This is Peter and this is Horatio. The girl is leggin'. Boys, this is Cap'n Smith."

The boys, not having hats to take off, gave slight bows and said:

"Good morning, sir."

Horatio felt this was not enough greeting for a man who had taken them all on to his boat so he added:

"I hope you are well, sir, and had a pleasant night."

The captain could not have been more surprised if a grasshopper had spoken. He opened his mouth and let out great roars of laughter. Presently he mopped his eyes.

"Did you get a load of that, mate?"—all canal boatmen call their wives mate—"Couldn't 'ave spoken nicer if 'e was the king hisself." Then he looked at Peter and let out another roar. When his laugh was over he gasped: "That's never the boy the rozzers is after?"

Seen in the daylight Mrs. Smith, though still enormous, looked larger than she actually was because of the fullness of her skirt and the height of her headgear. The trilby hat Margaret had noticed the night before was not her only head covering for she wore a rather battered straw bonnet with the trilby hat tied on top of it. Now in answer to her husband she nodded, which made the trilby wobble.

"The very same. Stole books 'e did, at least that is what will be said, but young Margaret says 'e only borrowed them."

The captain looked at Peter.

"An' what do you say? Speak the truth, boy. I won't 'ave no liars on my boat."

"Truly, sir, I only borrowed them. You see, one was

Bleak House. Well, I had to read it, you do see that."

The captain again shook with laughter.

" 'Ark at 'im, mate. 'E reads books! No, son, I don't see why you 'ave to read this *Bleak 'ouse.* I never learned to read and never felt the loss of it, but I can make me mark. Now see, boys, we don't want no sirs on this boat. I'm the cap'n and that's what you call me. For work you takes your turn as leggers. Seeing there's three of you shouldn't be too 'ard. While they're still out lookin' for you, Peter, none of you won't work no locks where there's a lock keeper. Ebeneezer or me'll do that. Me mate will show you about the tunnels."

He had finished with them and was turning away when he had another look at the green hair and the baggy suits. Once more he let out a roar of laughter. "If they don't beat cock fightin'. Couple of guys for Guy Fawkes's day if ever I saw them, then they open their mouths an' no duke could speak prettier. Take 'em away, mate, before I split a gut laughin'."

Margaret found that as she led the horse she stopped feeling sleepy so she was able to make plans. There were stables every five or six miles, Mrs. Smith told her, to which horses were returned and from which new ones were hired. But that did not mean their horse was returned to a stable every five or six miles; from what she had gathered about the unusualness of their being tied up last night and from what Jem had told her, she was afraid the poor horse often had an eighteen- to twenty-hour day and that meant so did the leggers—if not a twenty-four-hour day. Even dividing the day and the night into short shifts, could Peter and Horatio walk that far?

Margaret's thoughts were disturbed by Mrs. Smith, who came along the canal bank to join her.

"We're comin' to a tunnel an' I want to show you what you do so you can teach the boys."

Margaret looked at Mrs. Smith striding along beside her, her voluminous skirts brushing flat the young grass.

"Did you teach all your boys to be leggers?"

"Only me eldest, then 'e taught the next and so on down to Tom. They each started leggin' the day they was five. Mind you, when they was little 'uns I usually lent a 'and with the locks. They're 'eavy for small ones."

Margaret tried to picture the massive Mrs. Smith helping out when the work was extra hard.

"And for you, too, I should think."

Mrs. Smith hitched her brilliantly colored shawl more securely onto her shoulders.

"You're thinkin' I'm too fat for much work"—she slapped her thighs—"but it's not all me, it's me petticoats what makes me look so big. The cold is cruel on the canals of a winter and often into the spring. Last winter when it froze I wore nine flannel petticoats and three pairs of flannel knickers—me own, a pair what belonged to me ma and a pair what belonged to me old gran. Of course now the nice weather's comin' I don't wear so many, just the one pair of knickers, but I still wear four petticoats. Can't be too careful."

At the tunnel Margaret learned that she had to "unpeg" the horse. This meant untying his lead rope from the canal boat. Then she had to lead the horse along the bank to the other end of the tunnel and there wait for the boat to come through.

"But how does the boat come through without the

horse to pull it?" Margaret asked.

"The captain and Ebeneezer leg it," Mrs. Smith explained. "You can tie up the 'orse at the end of the tunnel. I'll send young Peter down, 'e can carry on till dinner time. When we say 'leg it' through the tunnel it means the men lie on their backs on two boards what are fixed to the stern either side of what we calls the stud. That's a piece of wood shaped like the letter T. Well, lyin' on their backs on these 'ere boards they push the boat through the tunnel with their feet."

"My goodness!" said Margaret. "Isn't it terribly hard work?"

"Shockin' sometimes," Mrs. Smith agreed. "You ought to see the Hare and Castle tunnel on the Trent and Mersey—three-quarters of a mile of it and bricks fallin' on the men, and many a time they've been stuck inside for as much as three days. They say motors is comin' to drive canal boats but I say so's Christmas. Well, you go on, dear, tie up the 'orse and show young Peter what 'e 'as to

do when 'e comes. Then it's on board for you to 'ave a bite of breakfast."

Breakfast was bread and jam and strong black tea.

"Meat's our food," Mrs. Smith explained. "Before a trip I buy a twenty-pound lump of beef or pork and another midweek. Then dinner time I puts it on the table. Then all on the boat takes their cut to suit theirselves, but it 'as to be enough for their dinner and their supper for they won't see no meat again till tomorrow dinner time."

Happily tucking in to unlimited bread and jam, Margaret asked:

"But why don't you put the meat back on the table for supper?"

"Because we don't. It's canal ways. Canal folk say sleep on a meal and work on a meal and that means meat. So afore we take a kip we eat what we cut off for our suppers and there's always plenty of tea and bread and jam. So come dinner time cut what you need and see the boys do the same or you'll go hungry."

That morning Margaret worked out a shift system. If the captain decided not to stop, each of them would walk the horse for four hours at a stretch. Horatio would do two shifts—eight to twelve in the mornings and four to eight in the evenings, which would give him plenty of time in bed. She decided she had better be the one to leg from eight to midnight because stabling the horse and fetching the new horse would come during that time. Her sharp eyes had spotted where Mrs. Smith kept the feed for the horses—chopped oats and bran—"and I bet I can sneak an extra bit," she thought, "so the horse doesn't go hungry to bed."

The first morning passed peacefully. If anyone was out looking for the children there was no sign of it for all they saw was a policeman riding a bicycle who never gave them a look. Then just before dark, as Ebeneezer was helping Peter with the gates of a lock, another policeman, this time pushing his bicycle, appeared. To the policeman's eyes, Peter looked like any one of the hundred or so children leggers he had seen at one time or another working on the canal bank so he didn't bother with him but addressed the captain.

"You seen three children dressed queerlike in orphanage uniform?"

The captain did not like policemen.

"No."

The policeman opened his notebook and read out:

" 'Two boys name of Beresford aged eleven and six and a girl name of Thursday aged eleven.' "

"No," said the captain again.

"What they wanted for?" Mrs. Smith asked.

The policeman did not know for Constable Perkins had not told him. But he was not going to admit that.

"That's as may be." Then he again read from his notebook. " 'The boys are very fair, noticeable so. The girl is darkish with curls.' "

At suppertime the captain was just going to take his first enormous mouthful of meat when out of the corner of his eye he saw Peter. Once more he shook with laughter.

"Mate," he said to Mrs. Smith, "I don't know what we let ourselves in for but I can swear I ain't seen no boys with noticeable fair 'air." Then he looked at Margaret. "Nor I 'aven't seen no girl neither."

Mrs. Smith laughed with him.

"Nor me." Then she turned to Peter. "You'll 'ave to eat up, young man, for it's time you was doing the leggin' and young Horatio was 'avin' his supper. And mind you don't speak to nobody for where there's one rozzer next thin' we know there'll be six."

In the Drawing Room

Lavinia was amazed to find herself in the drawing room where Lord and Lady Corkberry were having tea. Nor was she standing, as befitted her position, but sitting in a chair as if she were a friend of the family. Because she felt shy she stared down at the dirty little piece of paper on which Peter had written his message, though by now she knew by heart what was written on it.

"We kept it from you that the children were missing," Lady Corkberry explained, "because a nightdress from the orphanage was found in the canal."

"Our constable and the one near the orphanage thought it might be a case of drownin'," Lord Corkberry said. "Never believed it myself, of course. The police found nothin' and now this note proves there was nothin' to find."

"Have you any idea, Lavinia, where the children

might have gone?" Lady Corkberry asked.

Lavinia shook her head.

"No, m'lady. We haven't any friends in these parts nor anywhere, and anyhow I don't see how the children could get far in that uniform. I think they must be hiding close by."

"The police have searched pretty thoroughly," Lord Corkberry said. "Now suppose you tell us what you know about yourself. Maybe that'll give them a lead."

Lavinia pretended to have another look at Peter's letter.

"There's nothing to tell."

"But you remember your parents, don't you?" said Lady Corkberry gently. "Did not your mother ever speak to you about the place where she was born? Perhaps the boys might have gone there."

Lavinia again shook her head.

"They couldn't go there for it was in Ireland and she never named a place."

It was all Lord Corkberry could do not to give his wife an I-told-you-so look. Instead he asked Lavinia:

"What about your father? Was he from Ireland too?"

A slow flush crept up Lavinia's cheeks.

"We never heard him speak of where he came from."

Lady Corkberry saw that Lavinia for some reason did not like speaking of her father so she changed the subject.

"I wonder if Margaret Thursday has any friends?"

Lavinia's face lit up.

"Yes, she has, m'lady. She was found in a basket on the steps of a village church by the rector—not a poor baby for she had three of everything of the very best quality, and until last Christmas fifty-two pounds was left in the church each year for her keep."

"God bless my soul!" Lord Corkberry exclaimed. "What a romantic story! Do you think the little baggage made it up?"

"No, I'm certain she didn't," Lavinia protested, "for she told us a lot about that rector and about Hannah who brought her up. She loves them both very dearly."

"I suppose the orphanage would have their addresses," Lady Corkberry suggested.

Lavinia tried to remember all Margaret had told them on the train journey.

"The house she lived in belonged to two old ladies and it was called Saltmarsh House. I think she said Saltmarsh was the name of the village."

Lady Corkberry looked at Lord Corkberry.

"We had better send someone for the constable. He should hear all this."

Lord Corkberry nodded.

"I'll see to it. You stay here with her ladyship, Lavinia, until the constable arrives."

Lady Corkberry could see that Lavinia didn't like to think of policemen looking for her brothers.

"Do not worry too much, dear. I am sure they will be found in no time for, as you reminded us, how could they get far in those clothes?"

"What I'm wondering is, why they ran away," Lavinia said. "Margaret talked of it but I thought it was just talk. But the boys never thought of it and if they had they would have come to me."

Lady Corkberry wished that she could get on a more friendly basis with Lavinia. It was so difficult, she thought, to get confidences out of a girl who could not forget she was your scullery maid, yet she must try and get information about the orphanage.

"I had a talk with Miss Snelston this morning at the village school."

For the first time since she had come into the drawing room Lavinia smiled.

"The children say she is very kind. Do you know, her assistant called Polly Jenkin gives Horatio food. I mean she did give Horatio . . ." Lavinia broke off, her face crimson. What had she said? When the children were found they would, of course, be taken back to the orphanage and how much worse things would be for them if Matron found out there had been talk about how the orphanage was run.

Lady Corkberry guessed what Lavinia was thinking.

"I want you to tell me all you know about the orphanage for I can promise you it will not, when they are found, bring more trouble on the missing children. You see, I saw Mr. Windle today. He is a governor of the orphanage, as you know, and he tells me they will be delighted to have me on the ladies' committee. This means I can go in and out as I choose and I can assure you no child will in future be punished without my knowledge."

Lavinia looked at Lady Corkberry doubtfully. Could anyone, even Lady Corkberry, make Matron do anything she did not want to do?

"I suppose that might make a difference."

Lady Corkberry patted the seat beside her on the sofa.

"Come and sit here. I need your help, Lavinia. If, as I am afraid is the case, the orphans are neglected and ill-treated matters must be put right, and how can they be put straight unless people like myself know the truth?"

Once Lavinia started to tell Lady Corkberry about the orphanage she needed no prompting. She described everything as she had seen it from the first meeting with Miss Jones in the third-class waiting-room at Paddington. Then, having told all she knew personally, she repeated what she had heard from Peter, Horatio and particularly from Margaret.

"She's the one I heard most from because Margaret's not afraid of anyone—not even of Matron. I know she had all the punishments there are, beatings and being locked in a cupboard where there are black beetles and going to bed without supper. She was getting very thin— in fact, she looked quite different from when she came— but she never gave in and she never would have. I think she would have let Matron beat her to death first."

"And yet," puzzled Lady Corkberry, "she ran away. Why? What drove the children to do that?"

The butler, restraining himself with difficulty from a start of shocked surprise at seeing the scullery maid sitting on the sofa beside Lady Corkberry, came into the room.

"Mr. Windle asks to see you urgently, m'lady. There is a lady with him—a Miss Snelston."

Thomas Windle did not look a cold fish that afternoon. He looked what he felt—a truly worried man. He showed this by cutting out his usual formal manners and speaking almost as he came through the door.

"Oh, Lady Corkberry, since I saw you this afternoon about serving on the ladies' committee I have had a visit from Miss Snelston, whom I hear you know. Most distressing, most. If only the boy had come to me."

Lady Corkberry said:

"Do sit down, Miss Snelston, and you too, Mr. Windle. This is the missing boys' sister, Lavinia. Now tell me, you have some news?"

Mr. Windle looked at Miss Snelston.

"Indeed, yes. Tell her ladyship, Miss Snelston."

Miss Snelston felt in her pocket and brought out the message written on drawing paper that Polly had found in Peter's desk. She passed it to Lady Corkberry. Lady Corkberry read the message out loud:

" 'Miss Snelston M'am will you see these books which I borrowed get back to Mister Windle and oblige good-by Peter.' What books?"

"*Ivanhoe* and *Kenilworth* by Sir Walter Scott," said Miss Snelston.

"Both from my library," Mr. Windle stated, "and a third book is missing—*Bleak House*."

Lavinia said:

"That piece of paper, m'lady, could I see it?" Lady Corkberry passed it to her. Lavinia studied it. "Peter wrote this but it's not what he would say. I think Margaret told him what to write."

Mr. Windle looked unhappily at Lady Corkberry.

"Miss Snelston fears that these missing books are the reason why the children have run away. She thinks that they think I have informed the police that they have been stolen. Oh dear, if only the boy had confided to me his wish to read I should have been delighted and none of this would have happened."

Lady Corkberry turned to Lavinia.

"Has Peter had an unhappy experience with the police?"

Lavinia looked and felt shocked.

"Oh no, m'lady, he's just a dreamy boy always buried in a book."

"That is true," Miss Snelston broke in. "A most remarkable reader for his age. I allowed him to read in playtime—the children have little or no time to themselves in the orphanage."

Lady Corkberry was still looking at Lavinia.

"But if Peter has had no trouble with the police, why should he run away? Why did he not tell Miss Snelston he had borrowed the books and ask her how he should return them?"

Lavinia looked apologetic.

"I'm afraid he wouldn't have returned them until he had read them—books are all he cares about." Then, almost as if she had been there, she saw what must have happened. "I am sure it was Margaret who thought they ought to run away. Margaret makes stories out of everything. It would be just like her to think the police thought Peter was a thief and were chasing him. And she would have taken Horatio too because I'd asked her to look after the boys so she wouldn't have left them behind."

Miss Snelston nodded approvingly.

"That is what I believe happened, Lady Corkberry. Margaret is a remarkable child but, as Lavinia says, inclined to dramatize things. Now what I would suggest is that the police concentrate on larders. Although I am sure Margaret would not touch food which does not belong to her for herself I think she might steal for the boys."

"So you feel they are still in this area?" Mr. Windle asked.

"Positive," said Miss Snelston. "That uniform may be picturesque but it is also noticeable. Everybody around here knows the children are missing so one sight of the uniform and they will be found. But the police will have to have their eyes about them if they want to find Margaret Thursday."

Lavinia was not attending to what Miss Snelston was saying. Ever since she had been given Peter's note it had been nagging at her. There was something queer about it. Peter would not have fastened it to Wilberforce's collar for he did not know there was a Wilberforce nor to whom he belonged. Then it couldn't have been fastened to Wilberforce for long or it would have come off; that meant somebody must have had the note quite recently, somebody who, for some reason, could not bring it to the back door. But who?

Rain

From the beginning the captain could see his trip would have to be slowed down to fit in with the powers of his new leggers.

"Won't do us no 'arm, mate," he said to Mrs. Smith, "to take it easy for the once. If we works those boys too 'ard they'll only fall flat on their faces and then where are we?"

"They're triers," said Mrs. Smith, "no sayin' they're not, an' never a grumble, but you're right—it won't do none of us no 'arm to get a good night's sleep."

So a new timetable was arranged. The boat was tied up before midnight each evening and did not move again until after five in the morning.

The children were more thankful to work shorter hours, for though they walked slowly because of the weight the horse had to pull, before the captain tied up at night each had walked a considerable number of miles. Then there were the locks. Though Ebeneezer worked the locks where there were lock-keepers, to prevent the children from being seen, one of them had to run down and help him at all the other locks. And what a lot of locks there seemed to be! And what a weight the lock gates were! Even though they leaned on them with all their weight the children found them cruelly hard to move.

But there were compensations; they all liked the captain and loved Mrs. Smith. They tried to be friends with Ebeneezer but he, poor fellow, was weak-minded and had never really taken in that Tom was gone and the children had taken his place. Then it was glorious to eat as much as you liked. For the first few days on board Margaret and Peter could not take full advantage of unlimited food as their insides had shrunk while they lived at the orphanage, but when they caught up they made up for lost time, much encouraged by the captain and Mrs. Smith.

"That's a proper cut of meat." "That's what I like to see." "You'll never come to no harm if you looks after your stomick."

Another great pleasure was the tunnels. Often it took the captain and Ebeneezer a long time to leg through them. This meant that the legger had a lovely rest, the child stretched out flat on the bank and the horse quietly and gratefully nibbling at anything within reach.

"All the horses know about tunnels," Horatio told the others. "They always give me a sort of smile when we come to one."

Because they had to keep out of sight the children spent a lot of time on their bunks. This meant plenty of reading time for Peter, and plenty of sleeping time for Horatio. Margaret, after a rest on her bunk and perhaps a short sleep, would slip along to the galley to see if Mrs. Smith was there and, if she was, settle down for a talk.

"For she's the sensiblest person I ever knew," she told Peter, "even sensibler than Hannah and I never thought anyone would be that."

Except for the policemen and some lock-keepers, the children had seen few people on the banks since they came aboard. But there was another danger of which both the captain and Mrs. Smith were constantly warning them. This was when *The Crusader* passed another canal boat, which happened quite frequently.

"You see," the captain explained to the children, "all of us canal people know each other so it wouldn't do no good us saying we got three grandchildren on board because they'd know it wasn't true. Then if that rozzer asks them if they seen three children they wouldn't know what to say, see?"

As a rule there was no need to hide the children when a canal boat was passed because the two that were not legging were in their bunks. But they did have to keep a sharp look-out at the locks when one of the children was sent to give a hand to Ebeneezer. The danger was that someone might spot that the child legger was not Tom —but when this happened Mrs. Smith had a story ready. When two canal boats approached each other conversation started as soon as they were within hailing distance.

"How's thin's? What's your cargo?" Groans of sympathy greeted the news that *The Crusader* was carrying ironmongery for this was heavy stuff and backbreaking to unload at the journey's end.

As the boats drew nearer somebody—usually the woman—might look around and spot the legger. Then she would roar:

"That's never Tom. Who is it then?"

"Our Tom's along of Bert," Mrs. Smith would yell back, " 'avin' some schoolin'. You remember old Enoch what used to work for the captain when my boys were little 'uns?"

There had been an Enoch just as now there was an Ebeneezer, so often the woman on the other canal boat would help out. She would shout to her husband:

"You remember Enoch. Well, the Smiths have got 'is grandson leggin' for them. Tom's gone to get some schoolin'."

But the greatest pleasure of canal life, especially on the morning shifts when the children were not too tired to enjoy it, was the canal and the bank. Through the hedges they could see fields golden with buttercups. Each day they would bring back, like presents, news to the others of what they had seen. Herons, water rats, frogs, field mice, fish—there was no end to the excitements, and naturally each wanted to outdo the others. Peter, who from his first shift had realized you could not read and lead a horse, learned to be almost as sharp-eyed as Horatio and Margaret.

There was one thing about their legging the children

thought was a secret, though it never was for Mrs. Smith's sharp eyes had spotted what was going on. They never wore their boots except on the boat. Margaret had discovered that they couldn't on her very first shift. "Take off your boots," she had told Horatio when he had come to relieve her. "Hang them around your neck. As we mayn't wear socks you get awful blisters otherwise. Look," and she had showed him blistered heels. "But put your boots on again when you get on the boat for Mrs. Smith says canal boys always wear them."

Horatio had sat down and taken off his boots and had been pleased with the result.

"The grass feels all squidgy between my toes."

On the boat Margaret had given the same instructions to Peter.

"But for goodness' sake don't forget to wear them on the boat for Mrs. Smith says all canal men and boys wear boots."

Without any warning the children's pleasure in the canal bank came to an end. Mrs. Smith broke the news when she woke Margaret for the first shift.

"Terrible weather, dear." Margaret looked at her sleepily and saw she had discarded her gay shawl and instead wore a sack around her shoulders. Then she heard the dismal patter and gurgle of the rain on the cabin roof. "I got a sack you can have. It'll keep the worst off of your shoulders, but you'll all three have to share it as it's the only spare I've got."

Margaret sat up, took off her nightdress and pulled on her trousers. Mrs. Smith handed her her jersey.

"I know it's hard but you'll have to wear your boots today."

Margaret's head popped out of the neck of her jersey.

"I didn't know you knew we weren't wearing them. I get awful blisters if I put them on."

"You'll wear 'em and so will the boys wear theirs," Mrs. Smith said firmly. "It wouldn't matter who you was to meet this weather, they'd know you weren't no proper legger squelching along in the mud in bare feet. Now come and 'ave a cup of tea and I'll tell you how to cure blisters. What you want is hungry water."

Margaret followed Mrs. Smith to the galley.

"Hungry what?"

Mrs. Smith poured Margaret a cup of strong tea and told her to help herself to bread and jam.

"It's made of rosemary tops and home-brewed wine. Cure any blister, that would."

"Goodness!" said Margaret, much impressed. "I didn't know you knew about medicines."

"Bless you yes, ducks, all us canal women 'ave to. There's never a fine day but you'll see us on the canal banks picking what we need. 'Course a doctor's fine in an emergency and so's a 'orspital but they aren't always there. So us canal women makes our own medicines. Why, I never brew a cup of tea but I put in a pinch of hayriff."

"What's that?"

"Just a wild plant, but it keeps away the rheumatics. Then there's featherfew—wonderful for the liver and kidneys."

Afterwards Margaret swore that when that morning she fetched the horse from the stable and tied him to the boat she heard him sob. Certainly he knew how wickedly hard his work would be on so wet a morning, slipping

and sliding as he dragged his dreadfully heavy load.

"Be brave," Margaret told him, "and I'll help all I can. But it's going to be pretty awful for me too because I've got to wear my boots and that means blisters."

Margaret had a dreadful four hours. The wet grass slapped at her bare legs. She slipped and slithered on mud. In spite of the sack she was soaked to the skin and could hardly see where she was going for the rain cascading off the communal hat. But these troubles were as nothing to her heels. Very early on she had blisters, and soon at each step she felt as if a knife were cutting into her heels. She longed to take off her boots, but each time she looked at the boat she could see Mrs. Smith keeping an eye on her.

When at last Horatio relieved her, Margaret could have cried with thankfulness. But instead she nearly cried for Horatio. He looked so terribly small and already so very wet. She put the wet hat on his damp green hair.

"Oh, Horry, it's dreadful out this morning and your boots will hurt. If you can't bear it shout and I'll finish your time—I'm not a bit tired."

Horatio put the sack around his small shoulders.

"I'll be all right." He looked up at the black clouds overhead. "Perhaps presently the sun will come out."

Surprisingly all their blisters did get better soaked in hungry water before and after each shift, but the work remained desperately hard for it rained and rained day after day as if it would never stop. Then on the fifth wet afternoon, when Peter was legging, the boat just stopped and then crashed into the canal bank.

"Now then! Now then!" the captain roared. "What's to do?" He leaned over the side of his boat, peering through the blinding rain. "Peter! Peter . . ." Then he broke off to shout "Mate! Mate! Send one of the others to get 'old of that hoss. Young Peter's fainted."

New Plans

Peter was carried on board by Mrs. Smith and Ebeneezer
and laid in his bunk. Because she needed Margaret's
help, Mrs. Smith woke Horatio, who was asleep, and sent
him to look after the horse.

"You don't need to walk 'im, Horatio," Mrs. Smith explained. "Just keep 'im from chewing the 'edge. 'Is doing
that is what made the boat bump into the bank."

By now an experienced legger, Horatio, though half
asleep, picked up the communal sack and hat, put them
on and without fuss jumped ashore. There he pulled the
horse back onto the path.

"It's all right," he explained to him. "I don't mind you
eating anything but you must keep on the path because
otherwise the boat goes into the bank with an awful
bump."

The horse, grateful for a stop whatever the reason,
seemed to understand for he came obediently back onto
the path where he nibbled at the wet grass.

In the for'ard cabin Mrs. Smith was issuing commands
to Margaret:

"Get those wet clothes off of 'im. Put on 'is nightshirt. Cover 'im up good. I'll mix 'im a cup of tansy tea—rare tonic that is, 'ave 'im sittin' up in no time."

Actually Peter came round before Mrs. Smith was back with the tansy tea. He opened his eyes and stared, puzzled, at Margaret.

"What's happened?"

Margaret collected his wet clothes off the floor.

"You fainted so of course the horse went to eat the hedge which made the boat bump into the bank. That's how the captain knew what had happened."

Peter was surprised and slightly proud for he had never fainted before though he had read about it happening in books.

"Why did I faint?"

"Just tired, I expect. You walked a long way today because there weren't any tunnels."

Peter thought about that.

"Tunnels aren't much fun when it's raining—I mean it's too wet to lie on the bank."

Mrs. Smith came back with the tansy tea.

"That's better," she said, "though you still look as if you'd been dragged through a 'edge backwards. Now you feed 'im this tansy tea, Margaret, and see 'e drinks every drop while it's 'ot. I'm goin' to 'ave a word with the cap'n."

As the boat was stationary the captain was sitting under cover smoking his pipe.

"This is a rum trip, mate," he said when his wife joined him. "We started out to do a flyer in ten days, now the rate we're goin' looks like it might be three weeks."

Mrs. Smith sat down on a box of hardware.

"It's no good. I've known it was no good ever since the rain come—before that, really. I been havin' my eye on the kids, especial Peter. You can't see 'im proper on account of the walnut juice, but under it 'e's a shockin' color. Then none of 'em—not even Margaret—has ate their vittals right not since the rain come. They ain't used to it an' it's hard goin' an' that's a fact, though I never saw kids with a better 'eart for it. Never a peep out of one of them. We'll 'ave to let them go."

The captain was shocked.

"You mean give 'em to the rozzers?"

Mrs. Smith positively bounced on her box. It was such a bounce that the enormous earrings that she wore swung out from under the scarf that tied on her trilby hat.

"The rozzers! They'd send them back to that orphanage! Over my dead body. I reckon that matron is a real bad lot and I 'ope she gets what's comin' to 'er."

"Then what shall we do with the kids? If they can't do the work I'll 'ave to get another legger."

Mrs. Smith leaned toward him.

"I been thinkin'. Suppose we give Ebeneezer the leggin' and take on a new man to 'elp you."

The captain thought about that.

"Then what about the kids? We couldn't keep and feed them as passengers like."

"I got a better idea. Your sister Ida."

The captain had a great respect for his wife but this time he could not imagine what she was thinking about.

"My sister Ida! Why, I hasn't 'eard from 'er save at Christmas not in years. I wouldn't know where to find her."

Mrs. Smith felt in her pocket and triumphantly produced a Christmas card with a picture on it of a robin in the snow.

"I kep' it on account it's pretty." She opened the card and read out loud: " 'Doing all right hope this finds you in the pink as it leaves me doing panto as per for now but shall be round Chatham till June love Ida same address as usual.' "

"Chatham!" said the captain thoughtfully. "Chatham. Well, we 'ave to pass there but I don't see how we'd find 'er nor how she'd 'elp if we did."

Mrs. Smith had long ago accepted the fact that the captain took time to absorb new ideas.

"You forget the last time we see'd her. Lostock Fair it was. Remember what she said?"

The captain tried. Then he shook his head.

"No."

"She said not to forget if Tom, he was only a little 'un then, fancied a change as they had always a place for a little boy."

The captain slapped his knee.

"So she did. You thinking she might fancy Horatio?"

"Sure of it. Ever so nice spoken 'e is, and small, not much bigger nor a shrimp."

"What'll we do with Peter and Margaret then?"

"I reckon Ida will make room for Peter. I wouldn't mind keeping Margaret 'ere. Makes 'erself useful she does and she's comp'ny. The stories she tells—you did ought to hear 'er."

The captain saw no objection.

"How we going to write to Ida? Neither of us can write a letter."

Mrs. Smith got up.

"The kids can write—leastways Margaret and Peter can. I'll buy a piece of paper and a henvelope and a stamp."

Back in the for'ard cabin Peter had with difficulty swallowed his tansy tea, for he thought it was revolting.

"Never you mind how it tastes," said Mrs. Smith. "It's a tonic, which is what you need. Now I'm going to cover you up with all we've got so you sweat nice. That'll send you to sleep so I don't want a sound out of you till suppertime."

"But what about the legging?" Peter asked. "Margaret and Horatio can't do more than they're doing."

"Nor I 'aven't 'eard anyone askin' them to," Mrs. Smith retorted. "You leave the legging to me. Maybe the captain will tie up now seein' we've stopped—and maybe he won't. What you got to do is sweat nice and go to sleep."

Mrs. Smith and Margaret went into the galley where Mrs. Smith let down the table and put on it a bowl and one of her water jugs which, like the boat itself, was gaily painted with castles, roses and diamonds. Then she took off a shelf what Margaret had supposed was a white rope.

"What is that?"

Mrs. Smith poured some water into the bowl.

"A cow's tail, dear. We 'angs it aft for luck. The knot under it we calls the Turk's Head. It 'as to be washed reg'lar in pure water on account that soap turns it yellow. I suppose really it's the same as our paintings on this jug and on the boat, it's just for fanciness, but you won't see no canal boat what 'asn't its cow's tail aft and isn't painted pretty."

Mrs. Smith didn't like being interrupted when she was
working, so Margaret waited until the cow's tail was
washed and hanging up to dry before she said:

"Will Peter be all right to leg tomorrow? If he isn't I
could do some of his time."

Mrs. Smith sat down at the table and gestured to Margaret to do the same.

"Peter's not cut out to be a legger nor Horatio
neither."

Margaret was half out of the chair.

"But they can't go back to the orphanage for Peter
would go to prison . . ."

Mrs. Smith held up an imperious hand.

"Quiet now. Nobody hasn't said nothing about sending the boys back. What me and the captain 'as in mind
is the stage. The captain 'as one sister by name of Ida.
Well, she married away from the canal—and the fellow
she married is an actor—well, he's a bit more than that,
he's a manager of what they calls a fit-up."

"What's that?"

"I don't rightly know," Mrs. Smith confessed, "but
from what they said I don't think they acts in a real
theater, more fixes up a theater theirselves in 'alls and
that. Well, we think they might find a place for
Horatio."

Margaret had never been inside a theater in her life,
but she had touched the fringe of the theater world. In
her school several girls had collections of postcards with
photographs on them of the leading actors and actresses
of the day. Sometimes, as a great favor, she had been allowed to look at them. But she couldn't imagine Horatio
among such gorgeous creatures.

"I don't think Horatio can act."

Mrs. Smith knew no more about theaters than Margaret did.

"I expect he could learn same as he has learned to be a legger."

"But if we go to the captain's sister Ida who will be your legger?"

"We was thinkin' of makin' Ebeneezer the legger and gettin' a new man to work with the cap'n. And we was thinkin' maybe if I got paper and a stamp you'd write a letter to the cap'n's sister."

"Of course I would," Margaret agreed. "And you needn't buy a stamp, I've got two. I had three but I used one to write to Lavinia. I used to hide them in the toe of my boot at the orphanage but since I've been here I've kept them in my tin box that Hannah gave me. They are a bit scrumply and we may need extra glue, but they're still good stamps."

Mrs. Smith, inclining her head, accepted the stamp.

"There's a Tommy shop not so far along, we can get some ink and a piece of paper an' a henvelope."

Tommy shops catered to the canal boats. Margaret had not been in one because of the need to keep out of sight, but she had often seen Mrs. Smith go ashore to shop in them.

"Peter has a pencil. That would be better for I'm not so good at ink writing. Are you going to tell the captain's sister all about us? I mean about the orphanage and Peter having taken the books?"

Mrs. Smith did not believe in beating about the bush.

"We was thinkin', the cap'n and me, that Ida might want Horatio but she might take Peter as well. We was thinkin' you could stay along of me for . . ."

Mrs. Smith got no further than that for Margaret, her chin in the air and her eyes flashing, was on her feet.

"I don't care where we go but you're not dividing us up. Lavinia asked me to look after the boys and I said I would and I always will." Then Margaret ran around the table and threw her arms around Mrs. Smith's neck. "It's not, dear, darling Mrs. Smith that I wouldn't like to stay with you—truly I would. But I made Lavinia an absolute promise and I must keep it. Oh please, Mrs. Smith, do, do understand."

Good-by to Matron

Lady Corkberry was not the kind of person who started things and did not finish them. She had been prepared to find it hard work putting the affairs of the orphanage in order for she had expected opposition from the members of the ladies' committee. But as things turned out she was welcomed with open arms.

"Oh, dear Lady Corkberry," the chairman of the ladies' committee said to her, "how glad we shall be of your help. We—no doubt foolishly—believed everything that Matron told us and now look what's happened. She was so disliked locally that she was rough musicked by the village. The shame of it!"

Lady Corkberry and the chairman visited Matron intending to tell her that not only must she leave but so must Miss Jones. They found there was no need to say anything. Like most bullies Matron, when turned on, had become like a pricked penny balloon. All she could do was cry and plead to be allowed to go.

"It was horrible, horrible," she sobbed. "I could not believe people could be so cruel. Imagine rough musicking me!"

Lady Corkberry remembered what Lavinia had told her.

"You may leave by all means, in fact, we were intending to tell you to do so. But first there are things we want to know. Where do you keep the children's own possessions?"

Matron sobbed louder than ever.

"It's that Margaret Thursday. She has been talking. Nothing has gone right since that dreadful child came here. It's lies, all lies. I've not taken anything that did not belong to me."

But of course that story was no good for Mrs. Bones was still in the kitchen and, since she had always disliked Matron, was only too willing to tell tales against her. Soon Lady Corkberry and the chairman knew how much of the orphans' food Matron had not ordered so that luxuries could be delivered for herself, and how much good food had traveled up north with her each May.

"I will arrange for a conveyance to drive you and Miss Jones to the London junction this afternoon," Lady Corkberry said coldly. Then she held out her hand. "May we have your keys, please?"

Matron handed over the keys. Then she said, "What about our money?"

"That will be a matter for the lawyers," Lady Corkberry said. "I should not imagine you will receive anything considering how consistently you have robbed the children. You are a lucky woman we are not taking you to court."

Matron and Miss Jones left that afternoon at a time when the children should have been in school, but the children learned from Winifred what was happening. So, soon after afternoon school had started, without saying a word to Miss Snelston or to Polly, the orphans streamed out of the school back to the orphanage. There they hid in the bushes both beside the orphanage entrance and down the road. Afterwards Miss Snelston gave them a lecture on not being unkind to those who were already feeling low and miserable. But the children were not ashamed. Throwing everything they could lay hands on at Matron and Miss Jones had been utterly delightful and, though Miss Snelston might say they had behaved badly, the children knew they felt better inside because they had in a way paid Matron back for every moment they had been hungry and for all the punishments they had suffered.

Actually the orphans soon forgot the bad old days of Matron and Miss Jones. A new matron came whom they all loved, and so much money was raised by the governors and the ladies' committee that the food became wonderful—so wonderful that Miss Snelston had to organize extra games to prevent the orphans from becoming too fat.

Meanwhile the search for the children went on. The local police in Essex visited both Margaret's rector and Hannah, but they of course knew nothing.

"Margaret had stamps," the rector said. "I gave them to her myself. But she did not write and neither, to my grief, did I write to her. You see, I was told the authorities thought receiving or sending letters tended to upset the children so, much against my will, I had to accept their ruling."

Hannah surprised the police by the calm way she took the news that Margaret was missing.

"Margaret wouldn't have run away," she said calmly, "if there wasn't cause. But now she has run she wouldn't come here for she knows we tried every way to keep her. Very independent type Margaret is. When she's ready to tell us where she is we'll get a letter."

A few days later the rector received a letter from the archdeacon which backed up what Hannah had said.

"I hear from my brother, Thomas Windle, that the child Margaret Thursday and two boys have run away from the orphanage. I hear too that I owe you an apology. Far from the happy place I believed the orphanage to be, it seems there was a cruel matron—since dismissed. All is well at the orphanage now so I pray Margaret Thursday will soon be found."

"Pity he didn't find out about the matron before we sent Margaret there," Hannah sniffed, "but there's no need to worry. Margaret will be looking after herself and the two boys too, I shouldn't wonder."

Lavinia, too, was searching for the missing children, but her method of searching was different from that of the police. Hers was a question-and-answer system. Who on the estate would be afraid to bring a note to the back door? For days the answer was nobody, then suddenly she got a clue. One of the boys exercising a horse fell off and suffered a concussion. The doctor was sent for and it was decided that while he had to be kept quiet the boy should be nursed in the house. Talking of this to her staff, Mrs. Smedley gave Lavinia the clue.

"Her ladyship is too good the way she takes the stable-boys in. No reason they can't be nursed in their own rooms."

"I suppose there's no one to nurse them," Lavinia suggested.

"Nonsense!" said Mrs. Smedley. "Tough as old rope those boys are and what I say is, have them in when they're ill and the next thing you know they'll be in every day."

Lavinia was surprised.

"Don't they come in?"

"I should hope not indeed—only for the party at Christmas—I don't want a lot of stableboys smelling of horses in and out of my kitchen. Let one so much as come to the back door and he'd go away with a flea in his ear."

"So that was it," thought Lavinia. A stableboy! But which? Then she had her answer. Jem, of course. Who else had the children met? Somehow, she decided, she must talk to Jem. It was not easy for she had no excuse to go to the stables and when she met him it was by accident in the grounds. She had seen him on the day when Clara went to the dentist, but it was weeks since she had spoken to him. But now she had to find him however difficult it might be. "I don't care what happens to me," she told herself, "I must see Jem. I absolutely must."

The Tunnel

The boat was tied up beside the Tommy shop, and having watched Mrs. Smith go ashore to buy the notepaper Margaret went to the for'ard cabin for the stamp. Peter seemed to be asleep and so was Horatio, so very quietly she went to her bunk under which was her basket. She had not seen her tin box since she came on board for as she was happy she no longer slept with it in her arms.

Was it only in March that Hannah had said, speaking of the basket: "In a corner down at the bottom is that tin of mine with the cat on it you're fond of. I've filled it with toffees"? It seemed years ago and yet it was only weeks. "Oh, my dear pet!" Hannah had said. "Oh, my dear pet! You got some stamps the rector gave you. Bear it if you can, but if you can't you write and something might be thought of." Of course nothing could be thought of—Hannah had only said that to comfort her, but now that things were better should she write?

Sitting on her bunk staring at the tin box, Margaret felt such a longing to see Hannah that tears came to her eyes and trickled down her cheeks. She was brought back to the present by Peter. He was sitting up in his bunk.

"Why are you crying?"

Angrily, Margaret brushed away her tears.

"I wasn't. I never cry. Why should I cry? I'm Margaret Thursday and I only need me so I've nothing to cry about."

Peter was not a prying boy. Margaret had cried but if she said she hadn't that was her business. He turned politely to his own affairs.

"Can I leg tomorrow?"

"I don't think so. Anyway, Ebeneezer is going to do most of the legging."

Peter thought about that.

"But if we don't leg what are we going to do? They can't keep us here if we don't work because the captain only gets thirty-six shillings for a trip and, though that sounds an awful lot of money, it isn't really with all that has to be bought. The captain told me so. He said it was cruel hard to put anything by."

"We're not staying on the boat. Horatio is going to be an actor. Mrs. Smith has gone to get notepaper so I can write to the captain's sister about it. That's why I was getting out a stamp," Margaret told Peter.

"Will the stamp still work after being such ages in your boot?"

"I think so. Anyway the captain has glue if it won't stick."

"So you'll have one stamp left. Are you going to write to Lavinia? She would like to know Horatio is going to be an actor."

"I don't know. I should think it would be better to wait until we get to London. You see, when Horatio is an actor I think I might get a job as cook and perhaps you could work in a bookshop—at least you could if you don't take the books—and then we might have a little home of our own."

At this glorious vision Peter's face lit up as if he had a bright star in his head.

"Could we! Then we could write to Lavinia and tell her where we were and she could come and live with us."

Margaret was equally carried away. Of course that would be the right time to write to Hannah and the rector.

"And I'll write to Hannah and invite her and the rector to tea. Imagine tea in our very own little house!"

Peter came back to the present.

"I must be a legger until we get to London—do make Mrs. Smith see that."

Margaret was certain Mrs. Smith wouldn't let Peter leg. In spite of the tansy tea and a long sleep he still looked very peculiar. However, it was no good upsetting him so she gave him a nod, which might mean anything or nothing, then skipped off to the galley to write the letter.

The letter Margaret wrote was not well worded or elegant but no one worried about that. The miracle was that Ida, who had never been to school as a child, had picked up sufficient education since so that she could read a letter. Under Mrs. Smith's direction Margaret addressed the envelope.

"Put Mrs. Ida Fortescue."

"How do I spell that?" Margaret asked.

"I don't know, dear. How it sounds, I suppose. It isn't their real name, that's Robinson, but Ida says Fortescue has more class to it and it seems that matters to actors.

The address is a public house, it's called The Bull. They're so well known there I reckon if you just wrote 'Ida' on the henvelope it would find her."

To dictate, or what she considered dictating, was a great effort for Mrs. Smith. She untied her trilby hat and laid it on the table, which gave Margaret her first sight of the little black straw bonnet she wore under it. She put her arms on the table and, breathing heavily, said:

"Tell Ida that the cap'n an' me hopes this finds her in the pink as it leaves us. Then say the cap'n an' me is bringing you a little boy for an actor called Horatio. Tell 'er how 'e speaks very pretty. Then tell 'er the cap'n reckons he should 'ave discharged 'is cargo this next Saturday so we'll meet them in The Bull Sunday night bringing Horatio along of us."

"What about me and Peter? You haven't said anything about us," Margaret protested.

"Don't want to put Ida off, do we?" Mrs. Smith reminded her. "Bringing Horatio is one thing. Maybe she'll be pleased to have him. But tell 'er I'm bringing three kids and she mightn't show up at all."

In the end Margaret got a letter of a sort written, the captain provided glue to stick on the stamp and Ebeneezer was sent ashore to post it.

The next day, very early in the morning, the boat got moving, with Ebeneezer leading the horse. To Ebeneezer being a legger was a dream come true. He was tough and did not mind how many miles he walked provided no one asked him to think. Thinking was something Ebeneezer could not manage. Mrs. Smith, watching him, nodded her head understandingly.

"I reckon Ebeneezer will do all right with the leggin'," she told Margaret. "You can take over from 'im when he

needs a lay-off for his dinner an' that. Now what I want
you to do is stand by the cap'n. Help at the locks and
maybe 'e'll let you do a bit of steerin'. Of course, come a
tunnel you must take the 'orse from Ebeneezer so 'e can
leg through it with the cap'n."

Margaret did not want the boys to appear merely passengers.

"Horatio can lead the horse at tunnels. He likes doing
that."

"I got other plans for Horatio," said Mrs. Smith. "It's
no good my askin' Ida to take 'im for an actor with green
'air. I gotter work on 'im to get him back to fair before
she sees 'im."

The boys' green hair seemed permanent for all the
rain of the last few days had not affected it.

"How will you do that?" Margaret asked.

Mrs. Smith looked mysterious.

"I know 'ow. There's a wash my old gran made up.
There is camomile and costmary in it an' I don't know
what else but I got it all. When I've put that on the boys'
'eads a time or two there'll be no more green, I promise
you that."

Mrs. Smith's cure for green hair was not quick in ac-
tion. Twice that day and twice the next she made up a
paste and plastered it on to the boys' heads and twice a
day she washed it off. In between she covered their faces
with an ointment which slowly removed the walnut
juice.

Meanwhile Margaret was becoming a thoroughly com-
petent assistant to the captain. She saw a lock coming and
had jumped down and was working the gates before he
had time to yell for her. Under his tuition she learned to
steer and she was ashore and had hold of the horse at the

tunnels before the captain had time to whistle for Ebeneezer.

The day after Peter's fainting attack the weather began
to clear up, but by now they had left the real countryside
behind. There were still long stretches of green, and in
places there were fields of buttercups, but slowly London
was sticking out its tentacles, clawing in the countryside
in order to build factories and rows of sad black-looking
houses.

Margaret thought the change was horrible. She missed
the green and the flashes of gold where marsh marigolds
grew at the water's edge, but such things meant nothing
to Ebeneezer. He never looked right nor left but, sucking
a piece of grass, plodded on caring not at all whether the
path on which he walked was fresh young green or black
and cindery. As he walked he hummed tunelessly, which
showed he was supremely contented—so contented that
he was blind and deaf to other sounds. This was why,
when Margaret was having an early dinner in the galley
and the captain yelled: "Ebeneezer. Tunnel coming up,"
Ebeneezer heard nothing. When he was brought to a stop
by the tunnel itself he unhitched the horse and, forgetting that he should be on the boat, walked on with him
up the path to the far end of the tunnel.

The captain made such a noise shouting at Ebeneezer
that Mrs. Smith and all three children rushed out to see
what was wrong. The sight of the boys with their heads
tied up in towels made the captain madder than ever.

"Get down below, you boys. How do you know who's
comin' through the tunnel? One look at you and we've
'ad it."

"Skip it, boys," said Mrs. Smith. Then she joined the

captain. "Let Margaret run after him. She won't take long."

The captain leaned over the side of his boat to look at Ebeneezer.

"Won't take long! If Ebeneezer walks back the pace 'e's goin' now we'll never be unloaded Saturday."

Margaret had an idea.

"It's not a very long tunnel. Couldn't I leg through it instead of Ebeneezer? Then we won't waste any time."

The captain laughed.

"You leg it! Why, your little legs couldn't reach the tunnel side."

"You couldn't do it, dear," Mrs. Smith agreed. "It's dangerous. You could easy fall in, then like enough you'd be crushed between the boat and the tunnel wall."

Margaret was determined to prove not only her worth but that she and Peter and Horatio were proper canal workers. She stuck her chin in the air.

"Don't be silly! Margaret Thursday is as good a legger

through a tunnel as any Ebeneezer and so would Peter and Horatio be if you'd let them do it." She turned to Mrs. Smith. "If you'd let me put the pillows off my bunk on the boards they will lift me up enough for my legs to reach the wall. It's a very narrow tunnel."

It was a narrow tunnel and not long as tunnels went and the captain was in a hurry so, though unwillingly, he gave in to Margaret. Seizing the planks that were used for tunnel legging, he laid them across the bows.

"Get the pillows," he told Mrs. Smith. "Now come here, Margaret, and I'll show you how."

Margaret was never to forget that tunnel. Never could she have imagined how heavy a boat was to move when pushed along by human feet. Then it was so eerie inside. Icy cold water dripped onto her face. Bats flew so low she thought they would get into her hair. Even helped out by pillows it was all her legs could do to reach the tunnel wall. The pain in her thighs grew more and more excruciating. She was so intent on sticking it out and being every bit as good a legger as Ebeneezer that she did not see what every tunnel legger watched for—the pinpoint of light which meant the tunnel end. So it was a glorious surprise when suddenly the tunnel came to an end and the sun was shining on her face.

The captain helped Margaret to her feet.

"You're a rum 'un, Margaret Thursday," he said. "Pity you weren't born a boy—you'd 'ave finished up an admiral or such, I shouldn't wonder."

Margaret was pleased but she hid it.

"Thank you, but I don't want to be anybody but me. I'm going to make Margaret Thursday a name everybody is going to remember. You see if I don't."

All day on Sunday before they left for The Bull Mrs. Smith worked hard to make the boys, particularly Horatio, presentable. Their hair was now even fairer than it normally was and their faces quite clear of walnut juice.

"I would've liked 'oratio to wear a 'at," Mrs. Smith said with a sigh. "It would be pretty if he could take it off when 'e meets Ida and Mr. Fortescue."

"He'll bow," said Peter. "Mother taught us—she told us it was polite when you met a lady."

Margaret was once more dressed in her skirt and jersey but deliciously conscious that, because it was Sunday, she was wearing lace underneath. She was even more anxious for Horatio's success than Mrs. Smith for if Horatio were not accepted as an actor where were they to go?

"Do it now, Horatio. Show us how you'll do it."

Horatio got to his feet and stood in front of Mrs. Smith. He gave a beautiful bow.

"Good evening, Mrs. Ida ma'am. I hope you are feeling well."

Mrs. Smith was overcome with admiration.

"Oh my! Well, I never did! Oh my, isn't he the little gentleman!"

"Shouldn't he say 'Mrs. Fortescue ma'am'?" Peter asked.

"Rightly, I suppose he should," Mrs. Smith agreed. "But you do the best you can, Horatio. Why, I shouldn't wonder but what you was took on for the acting right away."

"What's to happen after they've seen Horatio?" Margaret asked. "Do Peter and I just walk up to you or do you call us?"

This was the part of the plan that was worrying Margaret, and she had reason to be anxious. After she was dressed in her girl's clothes she had repacked her basket and had suggested to Mrs. Smith that she should put in the boys' nightshirts, which were at that moment drying outside on a line. Mrs. Smith was usually a very direct sort of person so when she was indirect it showed.

"Well, no, dearie, I wouldn't do that. See, I don't know what plans will be made and it could be awk'ard if you was sleepin' in one place an' the boys another. No, I got a bit of paper an' I thought I'd make a parcel of the boys' thin's."

Now at Margaret's question Mrs. Smith again looked flustered.

"We got to see 'ow thin's shapes like. What the cap'n 'opes is that Ida or more like Mr. Fortescue can use a bright boy like Peter for takin' money an' thin's."

"But you will tell them about me, won't you?" Margaret pleaded. "I don't want any work. I'll get that in somebody's kitchen—but just to begin with if I could sleep where the boys sleep. You see, I did promise Lavinia . . ."

Mrs. Smith was clearly fussed.

"Now don't take on, ducks. I'm sure we can fix thin's up nice. But don't forget when we gets to The Bull you an' Peter sits one place an' the cap'n, me and Horatio another."

The Smiths and the children arrived at The Bull before the Fortescues, so the captain led Margaret and Peter over to a window seat.

"Now you two stay 'ere an' don't move neither of you till you're called." He had grown fond of the children, particularly Margaret, and felt worried lest they never were called. "Tell you what," he said in what he hoped was a cheerful voice, "what say I buys you both a bottle of ginger pop."

The ginger pop did distract the children for a few minutes for the captain did not bring them glasses so they had to drink out of the bottles. This was difficult to do for the bottles had been sealed by a glass marble in their necks.

"If only I could break this bottle I'd keep my marble to remind me of the captain," Peter said. "I think he's one of the nicest men I know."

Margaret looked at the stout glass pop bottles.

"For goodness' sake don't try and smash it, there would be an awful noise . . ." She broke off and gave Peter a nudge. "Look."

Peter looked, and both he and Margaret stared at what they saw. Mr. and Mrs. Fortescue had arrived and a very impressive entrance they made. Mr. Fortescue was handsome in a flamboyant way. He had dark curly hair and a most impressive mustache curling up at the corners. He was very grandly dressed, the children thought.

Mrs. Fortescue—or Ida as the Smiths called her—was even more grand. She had bright red hair on top of which sat an emerald green hat with a whole green bird on it. She was dressed in a green silk short coat over a long swirling dress. Close to, as the children were to find out later, the silk was cracking in places, especially where it fitted too tightly. The outfit was finished off by a high-boned net collar around which glittered what looked like a diamond necklace, and long kid gloves which had once been white.

Both the Fortescues paused in the doorway and only when everybody had seen them did they, with a start of apparent surprise, notice the captain and Mrs. Smith. Then Ida stretched both arms wide.

"Brother!" she exclaimed. "Brother, dear!"

The captain, looking embarrassed, came forward and gave her a smacking kiss. Then he turned to his brother-in-law and shook his hand.

"Well! How's thin's? What will you 'ave? The 'ospitality is on us."

Mrs. Smith, who was not the kissing type, pushed her brown cheek awkwardly against Ida's noticeably pink-and-white one.

"One moment, Cap'n," she said. "Ida and Mr. Fortescue will want to meet the boy." She laid a hand on Horatio's shoulder. "This is Horatio Beresford."

Horatio was perfect. He gave a beautiful bow before
he said:

"Good evening, ma'am, and you too, sir. I hope you
are both feeling well."

"If it wasn't Horatio who was doing it," Margaret
whispered to Peter, "I'd say he was showing off."

Peter saw what she meant but he stuck up for Horatio.

"He's only doing what our mother told us to."

The effect on the Fortescues of Horatio's politeness
was obvious. They looked at each other with faces which
clearly asked, "Would you believe it!"

"Speaks pretty, doesn't he?" said Mrs. Smith. "Puts me
in mind of the way you speak, Ida—ever so refined."

Margaret and Peter were afraid that everybody would
go to the bar where the drinks were served, which would
mean they would not hear a word that was said. Instead
the men went to the bar to fetch the drinks and Ida, in a

very grand way as if she owned The Bull, led Mrs. Smith to a table.

"This is our favorite," she said. "No one else would dream of sitting here when we honor The Bull."

The table was quite close to the window seat on which Margaret and Peter were sitting, so Mrs. Smith hurriedly pushed Horatio into the chair which had its back to them. He had been told he was not to speak or look at them, but there was always the chance that he might forget.

"Do you think you could find a place for Horatio?" Mrs. Smith asked.

Margaret and Peter now noticed that Ida, when not trying hard, sometimes forgot her elegant voice and talked more like her brother.

"Well, dear, of course I leave all business to Mister Fortescue. We 'ave—have plans for which this boy may be on the small side, but I expect we'll fit him in—mostly we can use a small child."

Margaret nudged Peter.

"If they want a bigger boy," she whispered, "I expect they'll use you. Would you mind?"

"I don't know," Peter whispered back. "I haven't tried but I'd like anything if only we could have our own little house."

The men arrived with the drinks and there was a good deal of raising glasses and health drinking. While this was going on Horatio, tired after the long day, went to sleep.

"I must say he's pretty as a picture," said Ida. She turned to her husband. "He won't cost much and he can make hisself useful."

Mr. Fortescue felt things were moving too fast.

"There's a play bein' made out of a book which I shall have the honor to present. There is a boy in it, but this boy is a bit too small for Cedric—do you not think, my dear?"

Ida nodded.

"I just said the same thing. Lovely play it is, it's called *Little Lord Fauntleroy.*"

"My public will eat it—just eat it," said Mr. Fortescue.

"And it might 'ave been written for us," Ida added. "There's the boy's grandfather, the Earl, and I think I say without contradiction there's no one on the boards today to touch Mr. Fortescue when he is appearing as a member of the aristocracy."

Mr. Fortescue gave her a bow.

"And the part of the boy's mother—Dearest, he calls her—fits Ida like a shoe."

The Captain cleared his voice.

" 'Ow old a boy was you wantin'?"

Mr. Fortescue gave his mustache an upward brush.

"Well, I'm not particular—he is seven in the book, eight when it finishes."

"There you go!" Margaret whispered to Peter. "You may be just eleven but you can look seven. Oh, I wonder if they'll mind me coming too."

A moment later Peter was called.

"As it 'appens Horatio 'as a brother," the captain said. "Peter, come here a moment."

Peter came to the table. He bowed to Ida.

"Good evening, ma'am."

Ida turned to the captain.

"Where did you find them? These aren't canal kids."

"Cedric to the life," said Mr. Fortescue. "But I tell you what, Ida—the little one will do for Tom, the false heir."

Margaret lost track of the conversation for a bit for first more drinks were fetched and after that the talk was about business arrangements. It seemed that both boys were to be apprenticed. She stretched forward hoping to hear what they were to be paid, but there was no mention of money, only "all found," which to Margaret meant a home and clothes and food. "Oh dear," she thought, "it doesn't sound as if we can have a little house just yet."

Presently the men got up to fetch yet another round of drinks, and while they were gone Mrs. Smith said:

"Ida, dear. Could you do me a favor?"

"If I can," Ida agreed.

"Well, there's a girl. She's not a sister to the boys but she's like a sister, isn't she, Peter?"

Peter was nearly asleep but he jerked his head up.

"Yes. Just like a sister."

"Margaret. Margaret," Mrs. Smith called. "Come here a minute, dearie."

Margaret slid off the window seat and came to the table. She gave Ida a polite curtsy.

"Good evening, ma'am."

Ida turned to Mrs. Smith.

"What d'you think we are—a baby farm? We don't want a girl. Six a penny they are. We got a girl workin' for us, well she's a grown woman really but ever so small she is, so when we want a girl kid she plays 'em." The men came back with the drinks and Ida pointed a finger at Mrs. Smith. "Thinks we're a baby farm, wants us to take this girl as well."

Mr. Fortescue gave Margaret a glance, then he handed Mrs. Smith her drink.

"Sorry, dear, but nothing doing. The two boys—yes. We'll have them tonight. The girl—no. Why, she's not even pretty."

He sounded so condescending it was more than Margaret could bear. Up went her chin and her eyes blazed.

"Thank you very much, but I wouldn't work for you if I was starving. I don't know who you think you are but I came in a basket with three of everything all of the very

best quality and marked with crowns. And every year one hundred pieces of gold money were sent to keep me. You may talk about me in a despising voice, but one day you'll be sorry because I'm Margaret Thursday who's going to be very famous. Just now I'm not sure how—I just know I am." Margaret meant to make a splendid exit, sweeping out of the public house slamming the door behind her, but she was prevented by Peter—a Peter she did not know existed, very pink in the face, his blue eyes looking as though there was fire in them. He flung his arm around Margaret.

"How dare you be rude to Margaret? We think her very pretty. And she's brave as brave. It was Margaret who arranged all about our running away and me and Horatio are not going anywhere without her."

In the excitement Horatio had awakened and now he decided to join in. He got up and came to Margaret and Peter. He caught hold of one of Margaret's hands.

"Don't mind that man, Margaret. Peter and me love you next best to Lavinia and we're going with you to our own teeny-weeny house you said we could."

Mr. Fortescue was looking at Margaret with a speculating eye. Now he turned to Ida.

"The girl's quite something when her dander's up—quite something."

Ida nodded for she, too, could see in Margaret what he could see. She turned graciously to the children.

"Come and sit down, dears. Maybe both Mr. Fortescue and me spoke a bit hasty." She turned to her brother. "I know you'll want to be making an early start so I'll just fix things up as best I can for tonight and tomorrow we'll manage something better."

Saying good-by to Mrs. Smith was to Margaret almost as bad as saying good-by to Hannah. She would have clung to her as she had clung to Hannah, but Mrs. Smith was not the clinging type.

"Good-by, dear," she said briskly. "I shall miss you. But we'll be seeing you all again soon. Send us a line, Ida, when you're acting this Little Lord Something and tell us where you'll be and me and the cap'n will be along to watch."

After the Smiths had gone the children stumbled along behind the Fortescues to their theatrical lodgings. Margaret was carrying her basket and Peter the brown-paper parcel containing his and Horatio's nightshirts and Mr. Windle's copy of *Bleak House*.

"Do you think it's going to be very terrible?" Peter asked Margaret. "I mean as terrible as the orphanage?"

Up shot Margaret's chin.

"'Course not. It'll be all right. Anything is all right as long as we stick together."

At Morning Prayers

In spite of all her efforts, Lavinia failed to find Jem. The truth was he was scared she might be looking for him, so if he went for a walk in the grounds of Sedgecombe Place he was as scary of being seen as a wild deer. Lavinia, though desperately anxious about the boys, did not know what to do. Everybody told her not to worry, the police would soon find the children, but first one week and then another went by and there was never a clue as to their whereabouts. Mrs. Smedley grew quite worried about Lavinia.

"You must pull yourself together, girl," she told her. "You don't eat enough to keep a sparrow going. Why, you're getting so thin one day you'll be going down the plug-hole with the washing-up water."

"Wouldn't you be worried if you were me?" Lavinia retorted. "I can't help thinking something terrible has happened to the boys and I think it worse in the night and then I don't sleep."

Though kind, Mrs. Smedley was brisk.

"That's being silly, considering the note Peter sent. Besides, worrying never did nobody no good. What you've got to do is stay where you are so the boys know where to find you, and keep your heart up. When you feel down try whistling—great help, that is."

Lavinia did try whistling and she struggled to eat her meals, but nothing helped. Then one night in bed she came to a decision. It was being stupid to suspect that Jem could help and do nothing about it—she must tell someone that she wanted to see him. But the question was who? The right way to do a thing like that was to tell Mrs. Smedley who might repeat what she had said to Mrs. Tanner, who in turn might tell Lady Corkberry. But it was such a vague way of getting anything done and there was always the chance that Mrs. Smedley, who thought nothing of stableboys, might not bother to tell Mrs. Tanner, which meant no one would tell Lady Corkberry. Unconscious that she had done so, Lavinia spoke out loud.

"But there must be a way. There must."

Clara was nearly asleep but she sat up with a jerk.

"A way to do what?"

Lavinia had a certain respect for Clara. Being a local girl with a mother who had at one time worked in the house and whose father was one of the gardeners, she had good solid knowledge of how the whole estate was run. Though Lavinia had never thought of it before it was just possible Clara might know how she could get hold of Jem.

"If I tell you what I'm thinking, Clara, will you promise not to tell anybody else?"

Clara saw no harm in that. Lavinia heard her spit on a finger.

"See this wet. See this dry. Cut my throat. If I lie. Now go on, tell me."

"You know that note I had from my brother?"

All the household and most of the outside staff knew the words of that note by heart.

"You mean—'dear Lavinia we are with Margaret and quite safe do not show this to anyone love Peter and Horatio'?"

"That's it," Lavinia agreed. "Well, there are two things about that note I keep thinking and thinking about. First, why should Peter write 'do not show this to anyone'? As he didn't say where they were going how could it matter who saw it?"

Clara sounded contemptuous.

"That's boys all over. Always being mysterious. I expect he just wanted to make it sound adventurous like."

"But that isn't what worries me most," Lavinia explained. "It's how I got the letter."

Clara did not follow that.

"I thought it was tied to Wilberforce's collar."

"That's just it, that is how it came. But you know Wilberforce, how he gets around. If that note had been on him long it would have come off so it looks as if someone had just tied it on. That would have to be someone who works here for if a stranger had come someone would have seen him, and if a stranger had touched Wilberforce he'd have barked the place down—you know how he is."

"Little varmint, don't I just!" Clara agreed. "My dad says if he was his he'd put him in a water butt."

"Well, I've been thinking," Lavinia went on, "and

I've decided it must have been someone in the stables and I think that someone is Jem. You see both my brothers and Margaret know him because he drove them to tea with Mr. Windle."

Clara did not answer immediately. Then she said, as if she were tasting the name:

"Jem! Jem!" If Clara could sound excited she sounded it now. "If Jem's had anything to do with it then where those kids are is on Jem's dad's boat. They're canal folk."

Lavinia had not in her wildest imaginings pictured the children on a boat, but now she saw that Clara might be right.

"The thing is I must talk to Jem. How could I do that? You see, I think he's hiding from me."

"You couldn't—not without saying why like. We aren't allowed in the stables and the stableboys don't come to the house."

"I know," Lavinia agreed. "I think and think of every way to meet and each day I don't. Oh, Clara, I'm so worried about the boys."

Clara was truly sorry for Lavinia and longed to help her. Probably it was the longing to help which made Clara suggest something which was far beyond what she would dare do herself.

"If I were you I'd tell her ladyship. I mean how you think Jem might know something."

"Would you? You mean ask Mrs. Tanner if I could speak to her?"

"No, not this time I wouldn't. You see, old Tanner's a nosey type so she would want to know why. If you told her why she might send for Jem who I reckon would just shut up like a rabbit trap. But if her ladyship were to talk to him that would be different. There isn't anybody who would dare not answer questions if her ladyship asked."

Lavinia decided her best chance of getting a note to Lady Corkberry was after family prayers. Now that Lord Corkberry was away prayers were led by Lady Corkberry. The staff filed into the dining room in strict order of precedence, led by the butler, followed by Mrs. Tanner and finishing with Lavinia. This meant that when prayers were over Lavinia had to open the door and hold it open until all the staff had passed through except the butler. He took over the door from her so that he might hold it open for the Corkberrys, who immediately after prayers went from the dining room to the morning room for breakfast.

"Somehow," Lavinia thought, "I ought to see a way to leave a note for her ladyship. Of course I'll be in real trouble if I'm seen, but I feel sure I'll find a way."

Lavinia had no notepaper but there was an exercise book in which Mrs. Smedley wrote down any special orders for the gardeners. The next morning at six o'clock when she and Clara came down to clean and light the stove, Lavinia tore out the middle pages of the exercise book where it wouldn't show and sat down to write her note.

"There's no ink," she told Clara. "Do you think her ladyship'll mind pencil?"

"May as well be hung for a sheep as a lamb," said Clara. If not comforting, this was at least common sense.

The note was short.

"My lady, could I see you on private business to do with my brothers respectfully Lavinia Beresford."

The note finished, Lavinia put it in the pocket of the clean white apron she would wear for prayers. Then, tying on her sacking apron, she got out her black brush and joined Clara at the stove.

It turned out not to be a good morning for doing anything unusual for Mrs. Smedley came down in a state.

"This is going to be quite a day, girls. Her ladyship had a telegram last evening from his lordship. He's coming home tonight bringing the Marquis of Delaware with him. Mr. Durham went off in the carriage right away to meet them."

Mr. Durham was the head coachman. Had he gone alone or had he taken a stableboy to help with the horses?

"Has Mr. Durham gone alone?" Lavinia asked.

Mrs. Smedley thought that a time-wasting question.

"How should I know and what business is it of yours, I'd like to know. Lucky her ladyship doesn't like much breakfast so there'll just be kidneys and bacon and the kedgeree. Get out the fish, Clara. You girls can give the men's rooms a lick and a polish today for there'll be a lot of courses for dinner tonight and likely enough very late so everybody get a move on."

Through prayers Lavinia had to sit on her hands to prevent them from trembling. Could she? Would she dare give her ladyship the note? Then prayers were over. Mechanically she got to her feet and opened the door. Through it passed the staff, the girls' aprons crackling, the men marching almost like soldiers. Then the butler was level with her and suddenly Lavinia was no longer afraid. She let the butler take hold of the door. Then, instead of going out into the hall, she walked across the room and laid her note on the Corkberry family Bible.

The Theater

Though they had slept on makeshift beds—the boys on a mattress on the floor and Margaret on a shiny horsehair sofa—they had all slept soundly, so they were in good spirits when they woke up.

The landlady where the Fortescues were staying was, the children thought, a very kind if dirty lady. But though dirty herself she let them wash in her scullery and gave them a splendid breakfast of sausages with fried bread.

"Eat up, kiddies," she said. "With theatricals you never know what time you're getting your next meal."

The theater was a tent which moved with the company from village to village. It was set up in a field. Outside it had posters stuck all over it advertising "The return by public request of Mr. and Mrs. Fortescue and Company, appearing tonight in that phenomenal success *Maria Marten* or *The Murder in the Red Barn*." In the entrance to the tent there was a wooden box rather like a sentry box with "Advance Booking" painted on it, but nobody at that moment was selling or buying tickets.

Inside, the tent was full of benches for people to sit on. At the far end was the stage with a rather torn red curtain draped on each side of it. The tent belonged to the Fortescues, the children learned later, as did the curtains, the scenery, the props and the wardrobe. When the time came for the company to move on, a farm cart and horses were hired for the removal.

Sitting on the front benches studying their parts were the actors, but they all got to their feet when the Fortescues came in. "Morning, Chief." "Morning, sir." "Morning, Mrs. F."

Mr. Fortescue went onto the stage.

"Morning all. Before we begin our labors I have an announcement to make. As you know, Mrs. Fortescue and myself have been desirous to add *Little Lord Fauntleroy* to the repertoire."

There was a murmur of assent from the company. "Until now," Mr. Fortescue went on, "we have been unable to commence rehearsals for lack of the right boy, but now we have acquired one." He looked at the back of the tent where the children were standing. "Come up here, children."

Peter seemed to be in a dream and Horatio was watching a butterfly which had flown inside the tent, so Margaret took them by the hand and led them to the platform. Mr. Fortescue patted Peter on the shoulder.

"Here, ladies and gentlemen, is little Lord Fauntleroy. Say good morning, Peter."

Peter, looking very thin in his too-broad suit, bowed slightly.

"Good morning to you all," he said politely.

Though it was a small thing to say it had a great effect for the tent fairly buzzed with conversation, all of which seemed to be approving. In a moment Mr. Fortescue held up his hand for silence.

"But Peter is an orphan and we must all do what we can for the fatherless, so I have agreed that Peter's brother Horatio should also join my company. He can play little Tom, the wrongful Lord Fauntleroy."

Horatio was an enormous success for he beamed at everybody and there were cooing sounds from the women of "Little sweetheart," "Little love."

Mr. Fortescue held up his hand for silence.

"One moment. These boys who were recently rescued from an orphanage so grim, so terrible I could not offend your ears by describing it found themselves a little mother." Mr. Fortescue laid a hand on Margaret's head. "Could I separate these babes?"

Horatio had been trying to follow what was going on. Now he looked up at Mr. Fortescue in a puzzled way.

"Margaret isn't our mother, she's our friend."

Mr. Fortescue gave a slight frown for he thought Horatio had interrupted a beautiful speech, but the company thought this funny and roared with laughter, so Mr. Fortescue decided it was time for work.

"That is all I had to say," he said grandly. "Now on the stage everybody concerned in Scene 1 Act 2 of *The Heart of a Mother*. And this evening parts of *Little Lord Fauntleroy* will be handed out."

Finding they were no longer wanted, the children wandered out of the tent into the field outside. It was a beautiful field full of ox-eyed daisies and buttercups with a hedge around it in which dog rose-buds were showing.

Peter had, of course, brought *Bleak House* with him and, since it was a lovely morning, lay down in the grass and was immediately oblivious of anything outside his book. Margaret took Horatio's hand.

"Shall we explore?"

Horatio had no time to answer for at that moment Ida came to the tent opening.

"Can you sew?" she called out to Margaret.

"Not as well as I can cook, but Hannah taught me to sew and we never stopped sewing in the orphanage."

"Good," said Ida. "Go round the back of the tent and there you'll find Mrs. Sarah Beamish. She plays character parts and sees to the wardrobe. You give her a hand and Peter can take on the advance. Where is Peter?"

Margaret pointed.

"Reading over there."

"Reading!" Ida was evidently impressed. "Fancy at his age! He shouldn't have no trouble then in selling tickets."

Margaret fetched Peter.

"You've got to sell tickets," she explained, "but don't fuss. Nobody's here to buy any so I expect when you know what they cost and all that you can go on reading until anybody comes."

Because she did not know what else to do with him, Margaret took Horatio with her around to the back to look for Mrs. Beamish. They found her in one of the two small tents which were used as dressing rooms. She was a short little woman almost as broad as she was tall, wearing a bonnet with cherries on it. She looked up as Margaret and Horatio came in. She had a surprisingly deep hoarse voice.

"There you are, luv," she said to Margaret. "If I gave you a cake of soap would you like to wash out Mr. Fortescue's things? There's a couple of pails of water outside. Pity to let a day like this go by and not wash anything—real drying weather it is."

Margaret preferred washing to sewing.

"I'd like to. Have you anything Horatio could do?"

Mrs. Beamish had very twinkling eyes, and now she twinkled them at Horatio.

"I want me cotton reels tidied—how about that?"

Horatio was pleased to help with the cotton reels so he sat down by Mrs. Beamish while Margaret went off with the laundry. Horatio rummaged through Mrs. Beamish's sewing basket.

"Do you want them wound up and the end put in the little proper place?"

Mrs. Beamish was pleased.

"Who taught you to do that?"

"It wasn't me that was taught," Horatio explained. "It was my brother Peter. Our mother taught him but I watched so I remember."

Mrs. Beamish looked in a puzzled way at Horatio.

"Did your mother teach you to speak that way?"

Horatio had found a reel of green cotton badly in need of attention so he was not really listening to Mrs. Beamish.

"What way?"

Mrs. Beamish felt around for the right words.

"Well—I don't rightly know—like a little gentleman."

Horatio nodded.

"She taught us everything. How to read—I didn't get far with that—and how to write. I can't do that either but I can draw."

Mrs. Beamish felt in her pocket.

"Like a cough sweet? Sarsaparilla they are. Nothing like it for cooling the blood."

Horatio politely took a sweet and put it in his mouth. He thought it tasted horrible. He was too polite to say so but he was not going to suck it.

"It's delicious," he said, taking it out of his mouth and putting it in his pocket. "But I think it's difficult to talk with a sweet in your mouth—don't you?"

Mrs. Beamish's eyes twinkled again.

"There's them as likes sarsaparilla and them that don't," she said. Then, changing the subject: "Will you like being an actor?"

Horatio looked up at her.

"I don't know. You see none of us know what an actor is. Even Margaret doesn't know."

Mrs. Beamish laughed.

"You will time Mr. F. has taught you. You must come along one day and see a play. We do a matinée Saturday. All about a Christian girl being thrown to the lions. You'd like that."

"I should," Horatio agreed. "You see, I never saw anyone thrown to the lions—in fact, I never even saw a lion. Where are the lions kept?"

Mrs. Beamish laughed so much she shook like jelly.

"You'll be the death of me! Lions indeed! Mr. F. has enough trouble paying all of us without feeding lions as well."

"But I thought you said I could see a Christian girl thrown to them."

"That's just pretending like," Mrs. Beamish explained. "All the men does a bit of roaring. Sounds fine."

Ida came round the tent with Peter.

"Where's the girl?" she asked. Mrs. Beamish explained about the washing. "When you're through with her send her to advance bookings. I want you to measure Peter. Mr. F. says we'll do *Little Lord Fauntleroy* week after next. You got that piece of black velvet I wore in *The Cry of the Heart*? Make him a nice suit that will fit. He also has to have a red sash and a lace collar."

Margaret was charmed with her job at advance bookings for very few people booked in advance—mostly they just came to the theater out of curiosity. So she was free to watch what was happening on the stage. And very interesting she found it. Mr. Fortescue, who swaggered about carrying a cane, was evidently a very grand sort of person. He was trying to persuade a girl to come to London where he could get her a very good job. As well as being the very grand gentleman, Mr. Fortescue was showing the girl what to do and how to say her part. She was a very short rather bulgy girl called Mary. Margaret could feel Mr. Fortescue was not pleased with her.

"Poor girl," she thought, "I bet she's the one who has to play children too, though I shouldn't think she ever looks like a child."

"Don't you trust me, my child?" Mr. Fortescue had to say. "I speak only for your good and for the good of your poor old widowed mother . . ." Mr. Fortescue broke off. "Come on, Mary, that is where you start to cry."

Obediently Mary cried—not very well, but Mr. Fortescue allowed her to go on.

"I don't wish to seem ungrateful, sir," she sobbed, "but my mother wishes me to stay at home."

Ida came onto the stage and dramatically flung her arms around Mary.

"I do indeed, sir. This child is all I have. Do not, I implore you, attempt to take her from me."

Mr. Fortescue held up his hand.

"Splendid, Mrs. F. Now, just to fix the scene, I will take it again from the beginning up to your entrance, Ida."

"Poor Mary!" thought Margaret. "I do hope she does it right this time."

For a while it seemed as if Margaret's hope had come true. But then they came around again to Mr. Fortescue's speech beginning "Don't you trust me, my child?" finishing with "your poor old widowed mother."

Mary seemed carried away by Mr. Fortescue's acting for she stared at him with a sort of blind look on her face. Margaret was feeling so sorry for her she could not help herself.

"Cry," she called out. "This is where you have to cry."

A sudden hush came over the theater. It was so quiet all those present could hear a lark singing as it rose toward the sky. Then Mr. Fortescue said:

"It seems I have acquired an assistant producer. I shall find more use for you, Margaret, than sitting at advance bookings." He looked toward the side of the stage. "Did you hear the child, Ida? We must consider how we can use her."

The Whole Truth

On reading Lavinia's note, Lady Corkberry took Lavinia into the morning room with her and told her to sit down. Then, while her ladyship ate her breakfast, Lavinia explained about Jem.

"I have kept thinking and thinking and yet I can't understand about that note I had from Peter. You see, Wilberforce is such a busy little sort of dog, the note couldn't have been on his collar long or it would have come off. Then who put it on his collar? It couldn't be anyone from outside so I decided someone who works here must have done it—someone who couldn't just come to the back door and give it to me."

Lady Corkberry was equally puzzled.

"Who could that be?"

"I couldn't think at first," Lavinia explained. "Then suddenly I knew. It must be Jem. You see, he knew the children because he drove them when they came to tea

248

with Mr. Windle. And if it's Jem they could be on his father's boat."

"Jem!" said Lady Corkberry as if she was trying out the name. "Jem. So you think Peter gave him the note to give you?"

"That's right," Lavinia agreed. "That's why I think he knows where they are. I've kept trying to see him but I have never had the chance. You see, we aren't allowed in the stables and Jem can't come to the house."

Lady Corkberry got up and pulled at a bell rope on the wall.

"You should have come to me before."

The butler came in.

"You rang, m'lady?"

"Yes. Send Henry over to the stables and tell him to find Jem and bring him to me here."

That was too much for the butler. It was, in his opinion, most unsuitable that the young woman from the scullery should be sitting in the morning room—but to bring in a stableboy!

"In here, my lady?" he said with all he felt in his voice.

"In here," Lady Corkberry replied calmly. Then she buttered another piece of toast.

When Jem got Henry's message he felt as if he had fallen down a rabbit hole so fast he had left his insides at the top. This was it. All was discovered. It was the end of his job, and the police station like enough for his mam and the captain.

When the butler, stiff with disapproval, had shown Jem into the morning room, Jem had known at once his worst fears were realized for sitting by the door was the girl he had tried to avoid—Lavinia. But Lady Corkberry was very good at putting people at their ease.

"Good morning, Jem," she said cheerfully. "Keeping well, I hope. No further trouble with your chest?"

Jem was so scared he almost lost his voice.

"Oh no, m'lady."

"I've sent for you," Lady Corkberry went on, "because we want your help. You did tie that note onto Wilberforce, didn't you?"

Jem went crimson to the tips of his ears.

"Yes, m'lady."

"So you saw the missing children?"

"Yes, m'lady—not willing, m'lady. That Margaret she came in the middle of the night. Proper taking she was in an' she'm say as how the rozzers—police, m'lady—is after Peter."

Lavinia could not bear the suspense.

"Do you know where they are now?"

Jem hesitated.

"Well, I do an' I don't in a manner of speakin'."

Lady Corkberry nodded.

"Quite understandable for I think in the kindness of your heart you hid the children on your father's boat. Didn't you, Jem?"

Really Jem was glad to confess everything for it had weighed on him, so he told Lady Corkberry and Lavinia the full story.

"I'd 'ave spoke up beforelike," he explained, "only I didn't want no trouble."

Lady Corkberry smiled at him kindly.

"There will be no trouble. His lordship is returning from Ireland tonight with Lord Delaware. I think they will wish to collect the children. Where should your parents' boat be at this moment?"

Jem reckoned on his fingers.

"It all depends of course 'ow fast they'm traveled—you see, the children isn't used to the leggin'—leadin' the 'orse that is—so it might take a day or two longer. But I would say the trip's over an' most like the cap'n's on his way back."

"Anyway, you know the boat and where it stops," said Lady Corkberry, "so hold yourself in readiness for I expect his lordship and Lord Delaware will want you to guide them and they will make an early start tomorrow morning."

Lavinia was so puzzled that the moment Jem had left the room she said:

"Forgive me, m'lady, but why wait for his lordship? Couldn't the police pick the children up?"

Lady Corkberry pointed to a chair at the table.

"Sit there, Lavinia. I want to talk to you. One day will make no difference. The children will be quite safe on Jem's father's boat for he and his wife are good people. I would not dream of informing the police who might blame them for what was intended as a kindness."

"But why should his lordship go?" Lavinia asked.

Lady Corkberry prayed she would find the right words to explain.

"Do you know what your mother's Christian name was?"

This was such an unexpected question that for a few seconds Lavinia did not answer. Then she said:

"Yes. It was Phoebe."

Lady Corkberry nodded.

"We thought it might be. You see, when his lordship

spoke to you one Sunday after church he thought he saw a likeness to your mother, whom he had known when she was a young girl. Then at Mr. Windle's he met Horatio and he was convinced. Apparently the likeness is extraordinary."

"Horatio is rather like Mummy looked," Lavinia agreed.

"So his lordship went to Ireland to tell your grandfather what he suspected."

"My grandfather!" gasped Lavinia. "I never knew we had one."

"I think you have. If his lordship is right your grandfather is the Marquis of Delaware so your mother was Lady Phoebe Milestone. She ran away from Ireland with the man she loved and your grandfather never heard of her again. What happened to your father?"

Lavinia clasped and unclasped her hands.

"We don't know exactly—at least the boys don't. I think he stole some money and used it to go to South America. I think Peter guessed something was wrong because the police came, but then Mummy got ill and that was so awful we forgot everything else. Then she died. At first I looked after the boys but I couldn't get work and that was when they got the boys into the orphanage. I never talk about it because, you see, we aren't really orphans."

Lady Corkberry did not like what she had heard of the children's father.

"I should not trouble your head about that. From the sound of things you are as good as orphans for I am sure your father will never come back."

Lavinia got up.

"You've been very kind, m'lady. Can I go back to my work now?"

Lady Corkberry got up. She came to Lavinia and put an arm around her.

"You may if you wish. I should have liked to have had you staying with me as my guest but his lordship—Lord Corkberry I should say—said you should be left where you were until he knew that your grandfather would acknowledge you. You see, he quarreled with your mother when she married your father."

Lavinia laughed.

"Me a guest! I couldn't ever be that, I'd feel such a fool—I mean they all know me as the scullery maid."

That night Lord Corkberry arrived with Lord Delaware. As Mrs. Smedley had expected, they were very late and demanded an enormous meal. After it Henry was sent to fetch Lavinia. Lavinia, at Lady Corkberry's suggestion, did not put on her apron or her cap, so she was wearing just the sprigged cotton dress she had on for her washing-up.

The Corkberrys and Lord Delaware were still at the table when Lavinia came in. She stood just inside the door smiling shyly. Lord Delaware, as if he were walking in his sleep, got out of his chair and came to her. He took her in his arms.

"Phoebe!" he whispered. "You're Phoebe come back to me."

The Rehearsal

Margaret became assistant to Mrs. Beamish.

"My old legs aren't what they were," Mrs. Beamish told her, "and there's a lot of gettin' about needed. Down to the shops for a piece of material, into the theater to fetch someone for a fitting and, of course, the everlastin' washin'."

So every morning as soon as the children got to the theater, as they had learned to call the tent, Margaret ran around behind to Mrs. Beamish and so did not see Peter's early rehearsals. Then on the third morning Mrs. Beamish, instead of giving her work, said:

"Sit down a minute. I got things to say to you."

Margaret knew she worked hard and as well as she could so she was not worried. She sat down on the floor and smiled up at Mrs. Beamish.

"You don't want me to tell you again how I was found in a basket, do you?"

"Not now, dear," Mrs. Beamish agreed, "though one day soon I will, for in the ten or so times you told me it's always a bit different, so I want to see what you'll make up next. No, it's on account of Peter."

"Peter! What's he done?"

Mrs. Beamish was repairing the dress Ida was to wear as "Dearest."

"It's more, from what I can hear, what he hasn't done. You know how it is in a stock company—you have to learn your parts quick or at least know the cues so you know when it's your turn to speak."

Margaret had not yet seen a performance at the theater as she and the boys were left behind in the evenings to put themselves to bed. But she had watched the company at work and knew that when they were not on the stage they were usually studying their parts.

"You mean Peter doesn't know his part yet. I know he doesn't and I am trying to help him. But, you see, we've not read the book and it's awfully difficult to learn things to say when you don't know what the person you're supposed to be talking to is talking about. All Peter has before he speaks is the end of what somebody says."

Mrs. Beamish nodded.

"I know, and I should by now with all the roles I've played, but it isn't just that Peter don't know his words— it's the way he says them, just flat off so I hear. And he don't pay no attention when Mr. Fortescue tells him how."

Margaret decided she had better be honest.

"He doesn't like acting much, in fact he doesn't like it at all."

"Beggars can't be choosers," said Mrs. Beamish dryly.

"Where would you three be if him and her hadn't taken you in?"

"Goodness knows," Margaret agreed. "Back in the orphanage, I shouldn't wonder."

Mrs. Beamish nodded.

"That's what I think and it's my bet that's where you'll all go if young Peter don't learn to act proper. It'll be no trouble—no trouble at all for Mr. Fortescue to send for the police."

The children were enjoying life with the theater company. They slept well, for though Margaret still used the sofa in the Fortescues' lodgings the boys shared a bed in the rooms of one of the other actors nearby. None of them minded being separated for the front doors were kept open so they could run in and out of each other's rooms as they chose. Food was irregular but they never went hungry for the actors were a generous lot and shared everything they had with the children. And one of the best things about the life was the permanent feeling it gave, for the actors were always talking ahead—"Next Christmas season." "Come next spring." "Might set up by the sea next summer." Now with one blow Mrs. Beamish had shattered Margaret's happiness. Mr. Fortescue might send for the police. Back to the orphanage. Back to Matron.

Margaret wriggled along the floor toward Mrs. Beamish.

"Oh no! No! Please—we can't go back to the orphanage, not ever. And Peter wouldn't even go there— you see, he took some books. It was only to borrow them but they don't know that . . ."

Mrs. Beamish stroked Margaret's hair.

"Now, now. Don't carry on so. I was only saying what might happen. Now I tell you what to do. You're as sharp as a cartload of monkeys so you slip into the theater and listen to what Mr. Fortescue wants and then you teach it to Peter."

Margaret jumped to her feet.

"Can you spare me now?"

Mrs. Beamish smiled.

"I did without you before you come so I reckon I can

do without you now. Not but what I won't say you are handy to have around and quick to learn."

Margaret went to the theater entrance. Horatio was sitting at the advance booking box. Not that he could sell tickets for he was no good with money, but he could call somebody if a customer came. He thought it terribly boring being tied to the desk so he was delighted to see Margaret. He slid off the seat.

"Can I go and play?"

Margaret put an arm around him.

"Not just yet, Horry. I have to watch Peter for a bit."

Gloomily Horatio climbed back onto the chair. He sounded sad.

"You know, Margaret, I liked it better leading the horse than sitting by myself out here."

Margaret slipped unnoticed into the back row of the theater. Peter, Mr. Fortescue and Mr. Ford, who was what Mrs. Beamish described as "The Comic," were on the stage. Peter, Margaret was sorry to see, looked as if his thoughts were miles away. It was clear from the way he spoke that Mr. Fortescue was losing his temper.

"This is the shop, Peter, owned by your best friend Mr. Hobbs. We have worked on this scene for three days and you still do not know when you come on, what you say or where you sit. What excuse have you to offer?"

Peter sounded apologetic, but Margaret was sure it was only because he didn't like to be annoying and not because he wanted to try and act better.

"Mr. Ford doesn't always say the same words."

Mr. Ford, though a comic, was a sad-looking little man. He was kindhearted so he tried to help.

"Look, sonny. It don't matter to you what I does before you comes on. I'm trying out some funny business with a bit of juggling, see, but I always comes to your cue and this is 'Shockin' what the world's comin' to.' Then you walks on all casual like as the guv'nor says on account you come and see me every day. You sit down on that barrel what is supposed to have apples in it, takes one and then when I sez ' 'Ullo' you says 'Mornin'.' "

Mr. Fortescue looked the way a rubber band looks when it is stretched further than it will go. He stared wearily at Peter. "Then you say: 'Do you remember, Mr. Hobbs, what we were talking about yesterday morning?' and Mr. Ford replies: 'We were mentioning Queen Victoria and the aristocracy.' Now that is where you show you are embarrassed—and when I say show I *mean* show —and then you say: 'And—and earls?' Now you do know why you're embarrassed about earls, don't you?"

Margaret was miserable for Peter's sake because she knew he had very little idea what the story was about. She clasped her hands and prayed, "Oh, please God, let him remember for I have told him about the earl."

Margaret's prayer was heard.

Peter, not sounding at all convinced, said:

"I suppose I don't want to tell him I am Lord Fauntleroy as he doesn't like earls."

Mr. Fortescue still looked like an overstretched rubber band.

"It is your grandfather who is an earl—not you. Now, Fordy, give the cue again and this time, Peter, put some life into Cedric."

It was no good. Peter did come on at the right moment. He did sit in the right place and he did take an imaginary apple but he could not act at all. He sounded,

Margaret thought, as a doll might talk if it could speak. It was just a string of words meaning nothing at all. And the worst of it was it should have been a funny scene. For Mr. Hobbs was so sure Cedric could not mean he felt him all over to see if he hurt anywhere.

was going to be an earl that he decided he was ill and All the way through the scene Mr. Fortescue looked grimmer and grimmer. Then they came to the line spoken by Mr. Ford: "Who is your grandfather then?" To which Cedric had to reply—reading from a bit of paper taken out of his pocket—"John Arthur Molyneux Errol, Earl of Dorincourt." As Peter was reading all his lines he did not pretend to take a paper with the name written on it out of his pocket, he just read out the name as he had read the rest of the part. This seemed to have the effect on Mr. Fortescue of a match on a firework. He jumped across the stage, seized Peter by the shoulders and shook him as he roared:

"You miserable boy! Out of kindness my wife and myself took in the fatherless and how are we repaid? By sloth, my boy, sloth. Three days and not one word have you learned. Moreover, you are stubborn. No child could be so deplorable an actor so I am forced to believe you are not trying. Go, Fordy, and fetch me a stick. I shall see what beating can do for this wretched boy."

Margaret acted without thinking. In a moment she was off the bench, and had rushed up on the stage. Mr. Fortescue had stopped shaking Peter but he was still holding him. Margaret put a stop to that. She seized one of his hands and bit it with all her force.

With a howl of pain Mr. Fortescue let Peter go. Then he sucked his hand where Margaret had drawn blood.

"You demon child! How dare you bite me?"

"I'll bite you again," said Margaret, "and I'll go on biting if you touch Peter. It's not his fault he can't act. He's going to write books and that's more important and . . ."

Goodness knows what else Margaret might have said for she was terribly angry, but at that moment Mr. Ford, carrying a little cane, came back onto the stage.

"Of course it's not my business, Guv'nor," he said, "but if I was you I wouldn't waste no more time on Peter. Let him help with the tickets and the scenery and all that." He made a gesture toward Margaret. "If you ask me there is our little Lord Fauntleroy. He's supposed to be a boy of spirit, isn't he? Well, she'll play him to the life."

"The Crusader"

The captain had managed to pick up a man to help him temporarily on board *The Crusader,* so with Ebeneezer leading the horse and the weather turned fine life was, as the captain put it, "fair to middling." In fact, his only trouble was that Mrs. Smith would, as he described it, "go on so" about the children.

Now that it was summer Mrs. Smith had taken off her trilby hat and instead wore a sunbonnet on top of her straw bonnet. She looked a shade thinner for she had discarded all but one of her flannel petticoats. She still wore a vivid shawl over her shoulders but it was made of cotton, not wool. Every dinnertime it seemed to the captain she started up the same way.

"I wonder what those kiddies are doin' now. I do 'cpe Ida has remembered what I said about Peter not being too strong."

The captain, cutting slice after slice for himself off the joint, would try and say something soothing.

"They'll be all right, mate. Livin' like lords they are after leggin'."

Mrs. Smith could not openly criticize the captain's sister but it was clear she felt uneasy.

"I suppose you're right but it's different for Ida never 'avin' 'ad none of her own."

"Now stop worriting," the captain would say. "It don't do your stommick no good worritin' while you're eatin' your vittals."

But Mrs. Smith did worry for she had become fond of the children, so she began counting the days before they were due back on another trip to London where she could visit them.

Then one day the Smiths had a great surprise. They were going through a lock when Jem jumped onto *The Crusader*.

The captain saw him first.

"Bless me Sunday trousers if it ain't our Jem," he shouted.

Mrs. Smith came out of the galley wiping her hands on her apron.

"Our Jem!" she said. "What are you doing 'ere?"

Jem looked around.

"I come—at least we all come to fetch the children."

The captain looked grim.

"Whatcher mean we all come? You brought the rozzers?"

" 'Course 'e 'asn't," said Mrs. Smith. "Don't talk so silly. Who's with you, Son? You see I got to tell whoever it is the children aren't 'ere no more."

Jem turned quite pale.

"Not 'ere! Where are they then?"

"They're all right," the captain explained. "Young Peter 'e 'adn't the strength for the leggin'."

"And young Horatio was too small really, not being

born to it like," Mrs. Smith added.

"Young Margaret was doin' fine," the captain said, "an' we would—at least me mate would've like to kep' 'er —but she wouldn't leave the boys."

"Then where are they now?" Jem asked.

The captain lit his pipe.

"You remember your Auntie Ida?"

Jem made a face.

"Don't I 'alf!"

The captain puffed at his pipe.

"Well, she married a Mr. Fortescue who is a theatrical man and 'e's got a comp'ny like."

"Give 'em a fine chance it will," Mrs. Smith put in. "You see, Mr. Fortescue is learnin' a new play what needs a boy like Peter to be a little Lord somethin' an' there's another boy wanted what 'oratio can do. There wasn't nothin' for Margaret but she wouldn't leave the boys so they kep' 'er like."

"But where are they?" Jem asked in a desperate voice. "I mean they got to be found an' took back."

Mrs. Smith looked flabbergasted.

"To that orphanage? Over my dead body."

Jem shook his head.

"Now listen, Ma. At the 'otel up yonder is waiting 'is lordship and another lordship from Ireland and Lavinia, the boys' sister. I didn't get a lot what they said but it seems the boys and Lavinia are the gran'children of the lord from Ireland only they never knowed it."

Mrs. Smith looked triumphantly at the captain.

"Didn't I tell you those boys spoke pretty as lords?"

"But, Ma," Jem persisted, "they're waitin' at the 'otel for the children. I been sittin' 'ere a 'ole day waitin' for you. What am I to tell 'em where the boys are?"

Mrs. Smith looked at the captain.

"We didn't 'ave no address like. You suppose The Bull would find 'em?"

The captain shook his head.

"Not quick it wouldn't. You see, Son, they don't act in a proper theater like. They travels their own theater and sets it down in a field. I know more or less where it is on account Ida told me so me and the mate could see the children next time we're down."

Jem made up his mind.

"You stay 'ere. I'm off to the 'otel to fetch their lordships and Lavinia—they best decide what to do."

In the end, because Lavinia had insisted on coming too, Lord Corkberry had decided they had better drive down to find the children. Jem, who had never lost his canal knowledge, worked out a likely spot where—even allowing for delays—they should meet *The Crusader*. Then, by inquiring from the various lock-keepers if *The Crusader* had passed, he checked his guess at a meeting place and found he was right. In order to attract no attention to *The Crusader*, the idea had been that Jem alone should fetch the children. They would then be driven back to Sedgecombe Place and, when they were safely under his roof, Lord Corkberry would inform the police that they were found. Jem's news about the theater was, of course, upsetting.

"We better go down to your father's boat," Lord Corkberry told Jem. "No good hangin' about here if the birds have flown."

"Never heard such a story in me whole life," said Lord Delaware. "Chips off the old block, my grandsons. Play actin'—'tis their mother all over."

Lavinia was the one who was upset. She had been so sure she would see her brothers that day. She was nearly crying.

"If Jem's father doesn't know where the boys are how can we find them?"

Lord Delaware had become very fond of his granddaughter. He put an arm around her.

"Don't fret, my dear. We'll find them if we have to comb every field that is lying around London."

In the end, of course, no one combed any field. For the first and only time in his life the captain turned *The Crusader* around. He found a place where the canal widened, and engaged a fresh horse on the opposite bank. Then the Smiths, Ebeneezer, the new man, Jem and the three passengers set off for London.

Curtain Down

A first night in the Fortescue company was a common event. For the more plays they had in their repertoire the longer they could stay in one place. But the first night of *Little Lord Fauntleroy* was rather different. The book had been popular not only with children but also with their parents. As a result, when it was known the Fortescues were adding the play to their repertoire whole families booked in advance.

"They are putting you in charge of advance bookings," Margaret told Peter. "Try and do it well because otherwise they won't keep you and that of course means we'll all have to go. I think you'll like it because nobody ever buys a ticket in advance so you'll be able to finish *Bleak House*. Mrs. Beamish says if I'm good as Lord Fauntleroy Mr. Fortescue is sure to give me some money, not enough to get us a little house of our own but enough to post *Bleak House* back to Mr. Windle. It will be a great relief to my mind when it's gone because then I'll know you can't go to prison."

Peter, curiously enough, did not mind selling tickets. He liked handling money and making sure everybody had the right change. And the customers liked Peter for they could be heard, as they walked away, saying to each other, "Quite the little gentleman" or "Gentlemanly boy, wasn't he?" These things, reported to the Fortescues, made them take a slightly better view of Peter, to whom they had scarcely spoken since what was known in the company as "the big bust-up."

The little impostor Tom in the play had almost nothing to say, but Horatio looked sweet and the company spoiled him—or at least would have spoiled him only he was an independent child who did not want to spend his time on ladies' knees or be given pickaback rides by the men.

"They treat me like a baby," Horatio complained to Margaret, "me what's been a legger. When I tell them they don't believe me."

For Margaret it was as if a door she had never known existed had opened wide. On the night when she knew she was to act Lord Fauntleroy she was allowed to take home the whole script of the play and read it. And as she read she found she understood Fauntleroy.

"It seems queer at first," she told Peter, "that he could think his grandfather nice because he was an old beast. But nobody had told him what a beast his grandfather had been so I think he truly got to love him."

Peter was reading his bedtime installment of *Bleak House* and did not want to be disturbed.

"I'm glad you like him and want to act him. I thought him an awful boy. Anyway, I don't understand about acting so I don't want to do it ever."

But Margaret did understand about acting as the company very quickly found out. There was no need to tell her that Cedric was embarrassed at having to admit to Mr. Hobbs that his grandfather was an earl—she was embarrassed and looked it. Nor was Margaret in the least put out by changes in a scene. The Fortescues knew their audiences and what they expected, so wherever possible they squeezed in a song, a dance, or some funny business for one of the cast. As Cedric, Margaret was an appreciative audience for all that went on, eating an apple while she watched and listened and applauding the artists when they had finished. But the moment Mr. Ford came back to a cue Margaret was ready with Cedric's next line.

"Proper find that Margaret is," Mr. Fortescue told Ida. "When she's grown a bit I can get rid of that poor Mary."

Ida liked that idea.

"Never had a mite of talent, poor girl."

Mrs. Beamish was given the work of transforming Margaret into Lord Fauntleroy. Margaret's hair had grown again and it now curled to her shoulders. One evening Mrs. Beamish came around to the Fortescues' lodgings with a large bottle.

"You got to be fair, dear, for his little lordship. This is peroxide. Come on, we'll give you a wash first and then I'll put it on."

For what seemed to Margaret hours Mrs. Beamish put peroxide on her hair with an old toothbrush. Then for more hours she had to sit wrapped up in towels while the peroxide took. But when the operation was over both Mrs. Beamish and Margaret were stunned with admiration. For in place of Margaret's brown curls there were now curls so fair they were almost white.

"Don't I look lovely!" Margaret gasped. "I always

wanted to be fair. Don't you think I look pretty, Mrs. Beamish?"

Mrs. Beamish kissed her.

"Wonderful pretty. And I don't mind telling you I reckon you'll never let it go dark again."

The boys were much less enthusiastic.

"You look like Ida," Peter told Margaret in a disgusted voice.

"You don't look real," Horatio said. Then he added doubtfully, "But I think I love you just the same."

On the first night of *Little Lord Fauntleroy* the tent had a full house for almost the first time in its history. Perhaps it was the full house or the thought that some of it was advance booking—but the company became nervous, and some of this nervousness was caught by Margaret who up to that moment had not known what nervousness was. Mrs. Beamish was helping her to dress. Margaret did not wear her black velvet suit with its red sash and lace collar until the scenes in the castle took place. For the opening scenes in America she had a frilled blouse and knickerbockers with a red sash and red stockings. Margaret gripped herself in front.

"Do you know, I feel odd here. Do you think I'm going to be sick?"

Mrs. Beamish laughed.

"Not you. Just a bit of nerves that is. Put one foot on the stage and it will all be gone."

What Mrs. Beamish said proved quite true. The moment Margaret walked onto the stage all the funny feeling was gone. But much more interesting was what took its place as the evening passed. It was almost as if the audience were holding out their arms to her. She could feel that they loved her—or rather that they loved Cedric and cared dreadfully what happened to him. It was a thrilling feeling.

Margaret was so engrossed by the scene in which Cedric first met his grandfather that she did not hear a slight commotion at the back of the theater. Mr. Fortescue, even though he was acting the earl, heard it, but when he saw that it was caused by more people squeezing in, it was good news so he paid no more attention.

What had happened was that Peter, counting the takings, was suddenly confronted by Captain and Mrs. Smith, Jem, Lord Corkberry, a strange man and Lavinia. He jumped out of the advance booking box, almost upsetting it, and flung himself on Lavinia.

"Vinny! Vinny! Oh, Vinny, we have missed you so dreadfully."

The strange man said:

"What's going on here? 'Twas said you were to be little Lord Fauntleroy."

"I was but I couldn't do it."

"Then Horatio is being the boy?" Lord Corkberry asked.

"No, Margaret is. Horatio is Tom, the impostor."

"We better go and see this," said Lord Corkberry. He laid a golden guinea on the desk. "Can you manage tickets for six?"

Peter shook his head and handed back the guinea.

"Standing room only and that's sixpence so I've no change for this."

"Keep it," said Lord Corkberry. "It will be a surprise for Mr. Fortescue."

The captain grinned.

"A surprise! Reckon it will give him the apoplexy."

Although none of them knew the story it was easy for the newcomers to pick up what was happening. The scenery was poor and makeshift and not in the least like what would have been found in the castle. The clothes, even helped out by footlights, were tawdry, and the acting, with a few exceptions, was not of a high standard. But the theater has its own magic and soon the Captain, Mrs. Smith, Jem, Lord Corkberry, Lord Delaware and Lavinia were as carried away as the most eager child in the front row. Even when Horatio came on the Fauntleroy spell was not broken for Lord Delaware muttered, when it looked as if Lord Fauntleroy was out and Tom was in:

" 'Tis a dirty shame!"

When the curtain came down Margaret found herself quite a heroine. Praise was showered on her by the company and very good to her ears it sounded.

The captain was sent around to the back of the theater to fetch the Fortescues. Like most theater people when a play has gone well, they were in tremendous spirits.

Ida gave her brother a smashing kiss.

"We never knew you were in front. What did you think of the show?"

"Never enjoyed meself more," said the captain. "Funny, I forgot the boy was Margaret really."

"Born for the theater," Mr. Fortescue boomed. "Born to it. Talent in her little finger."

The captain then remembered why he was there.

"You got to come and meet some people. Lord Corkberry and a Lord Delaware. Seems Lord Delaware is the boys' grandfather and he wants to see Horatio."

Margaret was taking off her stage clothes when Horatio was called by Ida. A very changed Ida who seemed almost shy of Horatio. She spoke in a cooing sort of voice.

"Come along, dear. There's friends to see you, bless you, and dear little Peter too."

"Dear little Peter!" thought Margaret. "That's odd. She doesn't think he's a dear."

Margaret was so curious about what Ida was up to that she hurried into her frock and ran through the theater to see what was going on. The first person she saw was Lavinia. It was a wonderful moment. Lavinia at last come to take charge of the boys. Until that second Margaret had not realized, much as she loved them, what a load Peter and Horatio had been.

Lavinia, hugging Margaret, said:

"Oh, Margaret! You've been wonderful!"

Lord Delaware came forward.

"So this is Margaret. You made a splendid Fauntleroy, my dear."

Horatio tugged at Margaret's arm.

"He's a lord and we're his grandsons."

"He's Lord Delaware. Our mother was his daughter, Lady Phoebe Milestone," Peter explained.

"And we're going to live in his castle in Ireland," Horatio added.

Lavinia put an arm around Margaret.

"And you're coming too, isn't she, Grandfather?"

"Of course she's coming too," said Horatio. "She's our sister now."

Peter smiled at Margaret.

"Of course you're coming too. We won't go anywhere without you."

Lord Delaware took Margaret's hands in his.

" 'Tis wonderful care of my grandsons you have taken, Margaret. 'Twould be a pleasure if you came to live with me. I would treat you as a daughter."

It was that word daughter. It hit Margaret as if someone had thrown a stone at her. A daughter! How could she be a daughter to somebody when she had a mother of her very own and was a person in her own right? Her chin shot into the air.

"Thank you very much but I don't want to be anyone's daughter. I was not found like an ordinary baby. I had three of everything all marked with crowns and each year lots of money was paid to keep me. I have friends, Hannah and the rector, and I've got a stamp so I am writing to ask them to come and see me act *Little Lord Fauntleroy*. And I have other friends." She smiled at the Smiths. "I could work on *The Crusader*, couldn't I?"

"Of course you could, dear, and welcome," Mrs. Smith agreed.

"It's not"—Margaret turned back to Lord Delaware— "that I wouldn't like to live with Lavinia and Peter and Horatio—I would. But, you see, I am Margaret Thursday and I'm going to make my name famous. I wasn't sure how but I think now it might be as an actress."

"Undoubtedly," said Mr. Fortescue.

"You show real promise, dear," Ida agreed.

Margaret looked up at Lord Delaware.

"You do see that I couldn't join somebody else's family —that I must be just me, don't you?"

Nobody answered that and yet somehow Margaret felt that they all understood and, in a way, approved. Then the captain said:

"If I 'ad a drink in me 'and I would say to you all:
'Raise your glasses, ladies and gents, to a girl of spirit—
young Margaret Thursday. May God bless her and good
luck go with her.' "